PRAISE FOR THE EROTIC ANTHOLOGIES
EDITED BY J. H. BLAIR

### The Good Parts

"If you ever flipped through a book looking for the juicy stuff, *The Good Parts* belongs on your nightstand. Fifty contemporary American writers . . . break taboos, quicken the pulse and make you sweat. All in one sex-filled volume."                          —*Playboy*

"A quality collection of beautifully written pieces that happen to be about sex . . . fascinating and revealing."        —*Publishers Weekly*

"Have fun."                                                      —*Detour* magazine

### The Hot Spots

"A broad, less strictly sexual definition of erotic defines this anthology. Its selections are nothing if not diverse, with vignettes that capture love among adulterers (Bliss Broyard), librarians (Aimee Bender), cybersluts (Martha Baer), hustlers (Scott Heim), and hookers (Laura Kasischke)."            —*Entertainment Weekly*

"An interesting array of styles and subject matter; everything from the subtle sensuality of the open road to the ever-popular loss of innocence is explored."                      —*Library Journal*

### ¡Caliente!

"A diverse mix of well-known and underexposed Latin American authors, among them Gabriel Garcia Marquez, Laura Esquivel, Reinaldo Arenas, and Isabel Allende . . . the stories are powerful enough to transport the reader to dusty Mexican marketplaces or steamy hotel rooms in Chile."               —*Library Journal*

*Titles edited by J. H. Blair*

# *Black Satin*

❖| CONTEMPORARY EROTIC FICTION BY WRITERS OF AFRICAN ORIGIN |❖

*edited by*

## J. H. BLAIR

BERKLEY BOOKS, NEW YORK

**B**

A Berkley Book
Published by The Berkley Publishing Group
A division of Penguin Group (USA) Inc.
375 Hudson Street
New York, New York 10014

This book is an original publication of The Berkley Publishing Group.

Collection copyright © 2004 by The Reference Works.
A complete listing of individual copyrights and acknowledgments appears on pages 179–82.
Cover design by Lesley Worrell.
Cover photo by Franco Accornero.

PRINTING HISTORY
Berkley trade paperback edition / July 2004

Library of Congress Cataloging-in-Publication Data

Black satin : contemporary erotic fiction by writers of African origin / edited by J.H. Blair.—Berkley trade pbk. ed.
p. cm.
ISBN 0-425-19616-X (pbk.)
1. Erotic stories, American. 2. American fiction—African American authors. 3. African Americans—Fiction.   I. Blair, J. H.

PS648.E7B55 2004
813.008'03538'8996073—dc22

2004041005

PRINTED IN THE UNITED STATES OF AMERICA

10  9  8  7  6  5  4  3  2  1

# ❦ CONTENTS ❧

Contents

# Contents

# ❧ INTRODUCTION ❧

IN DECEMBER 2001, ON MY WAY TO VISIT FRIENDS IN BUDAPEST, I stopped over for a weekend in Prague. Carp is a Czech Christmas tradition and the cobbled streets are full of barrels of fish. One of the barrel tenders was a young woman (punk haircut, brown leather jacket, I Love New York winter hat) who was reading (in English) a paperback copy of *An African in Greenland* by Tete-Michel Kpomassie. The book is the story of Kpomassie's childhood obsession with Greenland and the journey from his native Togoland to the icy north where he lives with the native Eskimos for two years. At the time, I'd already started collecting pieces for this anthology and the fact that a twentysomething in Prague was reading about an African in the Arctic seemed a particularly apt commentary on the rapidly growing popularity of writers of the African Diaspora. It is safe to say that at the same time the barrel tender was reading Kpomassie, someone in Tokyo was reading Toni Morrison, someone in Rio was reading

Charles Johnson, and someone in Bombay was reading Ben Okri.

In America it is in many ways a golden age of African-American writing. Walk into any bookstore in any mall and you're more than likely to find a well-stocked "black" fiction section that will range from the highly literary to the more immediately popular. There are innumerable book clubs, reading groups, and websites. In my native Manhattan, it's a common sight to see sidewalk vendors with a table of fiction, nonfiction, poetry, history, science fiction, and children's books. In academia, black studies departments are examining and exploring everything from eighteenth-century narratives of slaves who gained their freedom to nineteenth- and twentieth-century works by undeservedly overlooked authors. Many rediscovered writers are back in print so that a new generation can appreciate a Lloyd L. Brown or a J. Saunders Redding—to name just two.

So African-Americans are simultaneously writing today and rediscovering yesterday. And if it is something of a Golden Age, it should only get better. Just think of the young writers who have only started to publish in the last few years, including Colin Channer, Colson Whitehead, Danzy Senna, Edwidge Danticat, and Margaret Cezair-Thompson.

African-American writers are saying new things in new ways and much of it is extremely insightful and provocative. (For example, Colson Whitehead's debut book about the warring factions within the Department of Elevator Inspections is not exactly standard, run-of-the-mill first novel material.) Much of it is stylish, much of it is funny, and much of it is sexy. Which brings us to this volume. This anthology collects 30 excerpts from a wide range of authors to illustrate both the variety and the quality of erotic writing by contemporary writers of the African Diaspora. This book in no way pretends to be comprehensive. No single volume of this size could be. You would need at least five anthologies like this—covering the United States, Africa, Europe, Asia, South America, and the Caribbean. Even then, deserving writers would be left out. So think of this as a seriously sensuous sampling of diverse, dark delights.

And, getting back to *An African in Greenland* (which unfortunately has no erotica but does include wonderfully poetic evocations of ice and snow and nocturnal arctic mist), I've decided to include non-American writers. Besides, when it comes to writers (or anyone else for that matter) easy labels and quick classifications become increasingly silly and often downright meaningless. For example, is Jamaica Kincaid, who is currently living in Vermont but was born in Antigua, an American writer? Is David Dabydeen, who is currently living in London but was born and raised in Guyana, a British writer? How about Edwidge Danticat? She was born in Haiti but lives in Brooklyn. She grew up speaking French and Creole, but she writes in English. Is she a Caribbean author or an American author? (How about young, female, tri-lingual, Ivy-educated writer of lushly lyrical prose?) To repeat: This kind of classification becomes silly and meaningless. Akosua Busia (born in Ghana, educated in Europe, living in Los Angeles) is only too aware of this tendency to put people into boxes, to classify and shelve, to define and confine. In her novel, *The Seasons of Beento Blackbird,* her protagonist Solomon says:

> I've got all these cultures colliding inside of me and I'm sick of being made to choose. I'm sick of being treated like an outcast because of it. Here on the Island, I was made to feel guilty that I had an American father. Then in America, I was ridiculed for having a Caribbean accent, a Caribbean mother. And then I felt guilty that I grew to like America. I used to scream inside that you wouldn't come to live with me in the United States of "Babylon," as you call it. Well, I'm part "Babylon," Miriam. I can't help it! I was so grateful when I met Ashia; she made me discover the Africa in me but let me be all the other things as well. Not an American, not a Caribbean, not a black man in a white United States, but just a man. A whole man. She accepted all of me. I didn't have to define and confine myself. I finally belonged.

So this is an anthology of writers of the African Diaspora whether they're living in Lagos, London, or Los Angeles. And, just as this volume is a sampling, this introduction will be one, too. I just want to take a few pages and give some examples to illustrate the incredibly wide range of erotica being produced by writers of the African Diaspora. I'm going to start with sexual passion and rain. In these three passages the rain—and it's a different type of rain for each writer—is only briefly mentioned, yet is absolutely central to the erotic passion. My first excerpt is from Rosalyn McMillan's novel *Knowing.*

Taking the lead, Jackson eased Ginger back onto the bed, glided her knees up, then pushed them open like broken butterfly wings. While softly kissing her, he inserted one finger, a second, stretching her open for the third, inside the folds of her flaming lips.

As Jackson stimulated her clitoris, working his fingers expertly inside her silken casing, Ginger felt like an orgasmic butterfly, her breath like the flutter of wings soaring higher, higher and still higher than she could imagine, until finally, she cried out in painful ecstasy.

Outside, the wind sang through the billowing pines, the delicate tracery of branches brushing against the windows. Then it began to rain.

Sharp cracks of thunder couples with shrieks of lightning echoed in the sky above them. The rain fell in torrents while they made quiet love.

Moments later, the rain paused, creating patterns of moisture on the window, tracing, lacing lines of wet trickled down the panes. A small shelf of water buildup formed a ledge on the sill.

Still holding the keys to the melody, Jackson and Ginger embraced each other as if they were stepping inside each other's bodies. Like a mixture of gin and juice, the energy between them flowed from body to body as the suede smoothness of Jackson's penis pressed breathlessly inside Ginger as deep as it would go.

Like a dancer, he was in complete control, but knew how to lose himself in the music. He trained his mind to regulate the rhythm of his breathing with slow, deep breaths. With each stroke of his manhood, more pressing than thrusting, they moved together in concert. Together, with the thunder, the wind, and the rain, the orchestra was building between them. Her body was like music harmonizing with his, the melody, harmony, rhapsody building, and still building to an emotional peak, their consonances timbred. Their pleasure drowned out every sound but the music they heard inside their souls.

Pretty operatic/symphonic stuff, with melody, harmony, and rhapsody and especially "their consonances timbred." Yet it's okay because of McMillan's two lines about the weather: "Sharp cracks of thunder couple[d] with shrieks of lightning." Without the thunder and lightning the scene would seem overblown, overdone. But we all know the elemental fury of a raging deluge. A violent electrical storm elicits violent (electrical) passions and McMillan's lovers respond in kind:

> Bold with love, Ginger's moist fingers cupped Jackson's buttocks, pulling him deeper into her burning heat, loving him as he loved her. Their melded bodies moved provocatively, hip pressed against hip, gasping, in an accelerated rhythm. And their passion heightened with every crash of thunder outside. Through the pleasure and pain, the wind and the rain, their bodies shuddered. There was rapture.
>
> Outside, the beats of the rain softened, suddenly, then stopped. "Jackson!" Ginger cried out in ecstasy.
>
> He answered her with electric kisses on her lips before moving onto his knees and bringing her ankles over his shoulders.

Jackson gracefully kissed the spines of both her heels while tucking a pillow beneath her buttocks. Their bodies wet with sweat, Jackson easily slid inside her silken casing, and began rotating his hips, accompanied with equal beats of thrusts. Each gasp from Ginger fueled Jackson's desire to satisfy as he angled his hips from side to side, taking care to touch the outer walls of her vagina.

"Am I hurting you baby?"

"No, sweetheart. Please don't stop," Ginger whispered.

Ginger eased her knees up a little closer on Jackson's shoulders. She knew the sensation was heightened for him as she squeezed the muscles of her pulsating vagina. She pressed her thighs together, playing him like a precious Stradivarius.

They came together, she became him, and he became her. And then, she trembled.

Outside, it began to rain . . . again.

The second example comes from *Sugar* by Bernice McFadden.

Young lovers pulled each other closer, delighting in the pattern of the raindrops and the colorless day that looked in at them. Old lovers would once again feel the fires of passion and desire take root and remain tangled in each other's arms until night fell.

The rain had that effect on people.

McFadden never mentions the rain again (though she does tell us the bedroom has "the gloomy gray morning light"). She doesn't have to. We already know that everything else that happens in the scene happens against the backdrop of steady, all-day rain. This is totally different from the explosive, sudden storm of Rosalyn McMillan. This is a good old day-long soaker, with its dependable, reassuring pitter-patter. So when Pearl walks stark naked from the bathroom to the bedroom we can hear the rain. When she climbs in her bed beside Joe we can smell the rain, and when she initiates lovemaking we can taste the rain.

Looking up from the basin, Pearl caught sight of herself in the mirror and laughed aloud, a light silly chuckle reserved for soft young mouths of school girls just discovering the magic and mystery of a boy's touch. She cast a guileful smile at the cotton gown that hung expectantly on the back of the bathroom door and her eyes moved back to the woman smiling in the mirror.

After a moment, she flicked the light switch off and walked stark naked from the bathroom to her bedroom.

In the gloomy gray morning light of the bedroom, Joe lay on his side. His mind was slowly being pulled into the darkness of slumber and he barely heard Pearl enter the room. He would marvel later at the absence of the swishing sound that usually accompanied Pearl's entrance and the giggle that replaced it. He would enjoy recalling how Pearl climbed in beside him and pressed herself hard against his back, her legs thrown across his own, her breath, heavy with lust, against his neck. He would lick his lips in retrospect on the exact moment her lips brushed against the nape of his shoulder while her hand found the slant opening in his boxer shorts. He would not know that at the exact moment he realized his wife was naked against him and demanding in hushed, heavy tones that he flick her (those were her exact words) while she expertly guided his organ up and down between the soft palm and fingers of her hand, the memory of that moment would, for the rest of his life, dance across his mind causing a small smile to cross his face.

My third and last example of rain as integral to erotic passion is from the aforementioned Akosua Busia novel, *The Seasons of Beento Blackbird.*

Looking at the leaves waving under the pressure of the barely visible rain, Solomon could tell by the rhythm of their movement that it was about to come down hard. Stepping from the podium, he hurriedly shook hands with the Islanders who thanked him for his inspiring speech. "Please forgive me for rushing off," he beseeched the crowd as he sprinted across the rain-softened soil and leaped onto his waiting motorbike.

Roaring along the isolated sandy coast toward Miriam's adobe, Solomon called out her name to the crashing waves. "Miriaaaam!" he bellowed—an incantation—his voice scattering through the wind like confetti over a bride. Rapt by his impassioned cry, migrating seabirds lost their formation, regrouped, and fluttered higher into the sky. Solomon leaned his bike acutely to the left, his body precariously close to the ground. The sense of danger gave his voice more power. "Miriaaaam!" he bellowed again, spreading his arms fullstretch as the wings of the seabirds flying up above. The wheels of his motorbike spun almost out of control, and he laughed, grabbed the handlebars, sloped to the left, and accelerated.

\*    \*    \*

Alone in the quiet of her kitchen, Miriam sat at the wooden table peeling away the orange-yellow skins of overripe mangoes piled high on a plate in preparation for boiling. Their delectable aroma hung in the air. She licked the sticky sweetness off her fingers as she worked, her soft pink tongue catching the runaway juice that occasionally dribbled down her palm onto her wrist. Glancing toward the big bay windows, she saw for the first time the light rain that was falling silently from the sky.

In these three paragraphs we get nothing explicitly sexual and not all that much in the way of rain description either. Yet we know that what will follow—the lovemaking between Solomon and Miriam—will be, just like the imminent storm, very passionate and very strong. How do we know this? Because of Busia's selection of key descriptive details. We know Solomon is a keen nature observer. He can tell by the rhythm of the waving leaves that "it was about to come down hard." So he races off on his motorbike to beat the rain, to get to Miriam so they can be making love during the ensuing downpour. He calls out Miriam's name to the waves and drives too fast but the "sense of danger gave his voice more power." When his bike "spun almost out of control," he laughed and accelerated. In other words, Solomon is both a deep appreciator of nature and an exuberant (and playful) lover of complete exhilaration. He is not afraid of danger, and has complete confidence in his ability to handle that danger. For her part, we know that Miriam is a sensual woman. Peeling mangoes is not work, not kitchen drudgery, but is actually more like a form of foreplay as she revels in the "delectable aroma" and "lick[s] the sticky sweetness off her fingers . . . her soft pink tongue catching the runaway juice." Busia doesn't have to write one more word about what will happen. She has given us smells, tastes, colors, and exhilaration (plus fluttering seabirds and crashing waves) as a strongly sensual foreshadowing of the passion Solomon and Miriam will share.

Now, leaving the rain but staying with Akosua Busia, here is a brief excerpt that perfectly illustrates the sensory newness that writers of the African Diaspora are bringing to erotic writing.

Olu opened the door with his key. The best part about entering Ashia's apartment was the smells. First there was the constant aroma of cooking. Ashia loved the steadiness of a low oven, so she baked everything for hours, causing the aromas to ooze out slowly and linger long. Soft plantain bread and roasted peanuts. Cassava leaf stew in red palm oil. Rosemary chicken smothered in dried shrimp pepper. Yellow pound cake with lemon butter icing. Then there was the powdered fragrance of Amankwa, the

cleanest little infant in the universe. That munchy-baby-toe-
sucking clean that only scrubbed little children can produce.
Then, of course, there was Ashia herself. . . .

Olu inhaled deep, trying to hold in the intoxicating scent of
her silky dark skin oiled with sandalwood, cedarwood, lavender,
and a touch of patchouli. Ahh . . . He let out a breath and inhaled her soft cocoa-butter hands, the coconut oil of her long
black braids, and ahh . . . mmmmm . . . her full, plump, succulent, nibble-them-up, mint-tingle lips.

A sensory feast in less than two hundred words. She starts with
cooking smells and ends with Ashia's own lips being described
as a culinary delicacy, "full, plump, succulent, nibble-them-up,
mint-tingle lips." Lots of first-rate (and some not-so-first-rate) fiction writers combine food and erotica. It's almost a prerequisite for
Latin American authors. What's new and different here is the way
Busia inserts the smell of the baby between food and female.
Most writers would go straight from the "yellow pound cake with
lemon butter icing" to "the intoxicating scent of her silky dark
skin." "That munchy-baby-toe-sucking clean" is just the right
touch to set this apart, to make it unique from the many sensu-
ously written yet more standard couplings of food and female.

Another quick example of something absolutely new when it
comes to writing sensuality can be found in the way Dionne
Brand starts her 1999 novel, *At the Full and Change of the
Moon.* The book begins on the island of Trinidad in 1824.
Marie Ursule is leader and priestess of a secret society of militant

slaves called the Sans Peur Regiment. On the very first page she has gathered poisons for a mass suicide.

> Marie Ursule woke up this morning knowing what morning it was and that it might be her last.
>
> She had gathered the poisons the way anyone else might gather flowers, the way one gathers scents or small wishes and fondnesses. Gathering a bit here, wondering at a fiercely beautiful flower there. Tasting the waxiness of some leaves, putting her tongue on the prickliness or roughness of others. And she had been diligent and faithful the way any collector would be, any fervent lover. Scientific. Passionate. Every new knowledge, wonderful. She had even felt the knowing sadness, the melancholy that lovers feel, the haunting not-enough feeling, the way one covets the flight of swifts and terns and nightjars. She had sorted out the most benign vines from the most potent, collecting them all, and anything else she could find, recognizing the leaves through resemblance or smell or bitterness.

Some people might not consider this erotica per se, but I think it's erotic writing of the highest order. Not only does she gather poisons the way most people gather flowers, but Brand compares her to "any fervent lover." She has exhibited all the best qualities of someone in love. She is "diligent," "faithful," "scientific," and "passionate." And with "every new knowledge" comes wonder. Brand also tells us—and this is both beautiful and deep—that "she had even felt the knowing sadness, the melancholy that lovers feel." This is absolutely exquisite prose. Her word selection is perfect, as when she matches the words "gathering . . . wondering . . . tasting," and when she uses the flawless and poetic "swifts and terns and nightjars." Very sexy. Very sad.

\* \* \*

And now for something completely different. To go from the very sensual (and very female) to the very graphic (and very male). The following is from Clarence Major's novel *All-Night Visitors*, finally reissued a few years ago the way the author intended it to be. Many people call it one of the best first novels ever written. True. But I would go further. I would call it one of the dozen best American novels of the 1960s. The book is full of graphic sex. Much of it is desperate sex. But it's incredibly complex, deeply thoughtful sex. Major's writing is intensity plus intellectuality.

> For the first time I'm getting really into Cathy's delicate, tense, *ekundu-eupe* cunt, the sweet tight valley of its fruit, I taste with the string end of my velvet-tipped, busy tongue, we are at last deep in a frenzy, slimy with our own juices, in the big bed, here in the darkness, the winter coolness, her large clean smooth cheeks, I hold wide apart, she is meanwhile nibbling at the glossy head of my screwdriver, this *bisfisi* object new in her mouth, in her virgin body. I have her going for the first time, really relaxing, her oven is tense with pleasure under the prodding of my persistent tongue, and she is twisting, her hole forming an O, it is so tense with the pleasure, the *shimo ma* of her so beautiful!

Major is so good at this; he makes it seem easy. He gives us *"ekundu-eupe," "bisfisi,"* and *"shimo ma,"* along with the more traditional "sweet . . . valley . . . fruit." "Winter coolness" is accompanied with "frenzy." Writing like this is a delicate balancing act and yet he makes it read so easily.

> I watch it, watch the pussy *bokoboko* flow out, a fruit ripe with the intensity of my expert masterwork, the nest of her—about to give birth to a vast!—choking—bubbling fluid *ass deluge!* I can tell, the outer lips are puckered, swollen tense, she is groaning—her other mouth accidentally biting my dick in excitement; her sheath is jerking in spasms!—her buttocks can't stay restful. She dislodges my member from her mouth. *Fimbo!* Too much for her, at last!

Again his totally unique, individualistic word selection: *"bokoboko"* in the same sentence as "intensity of my expert masterwork"; "vast" and "sheath" as well as "ass deluge" and *"fimbo."* And this is how he finishes:

> I'm going very gently, now knowing that it is too much to take lightly. I let my tongue simply glide over the silky surface of her stiff clitoris, the lips are still so tense that I know too much pressure from me would make her jump out of her golden age, her honey days, her palmy age.
>
> I hold her ass *(punda)* as it is trembling in *so* much ecstasy.
>
> Meanwhile, I am becoming irritated and annoyed with her because she has completely forgotten my selfish and lonely,

throbbing *cokke*. The fluid flows smoothly down the pink crack
of her *matako*; I'm not going to let her stop me *this* time —

I'm going to carry her — carry her all the way — all the way to
the end. The end of herself. Into herself! Where she will empty
into her first complete orgasm.

I'm going to end this brief intro with a quiz: five passages from
five different writers that will help illustrate my point about the
quality and variety of erotica that has been and is being produced by writers of the African Diaspora. See how many of the
authors you can identify.

I'll give you a clue for the first one. It's from 1947. It's also —
as far as I know — the first nude, interracial cooking and eating
scene in American literature.

### #1

Now barefooted and nude and dripping, leaving footprints across
the floor, they went into the kitchen and scrambled eggs and
cooked hamburger patties rare with brown sugar sprinkled on
them. She split a loaf of French sour-dough bread, rubbed it with
garlic, spread butter on it, and put it in the oven so the butter
would melt. He washed and sliced onions and found mustard and
green peppers. They put their chairs together so their legs could
touch, and ate garlic bread, scrambled eggs, and rare hamburger
patties sprinkled with brown sugar and spread with mustard and
onions and peppers, and drank sour claret wine. And it tasted
more delicious than anything they'd ever eaten in all their lives.

From each other's mouths they took the food like children, and to each it tasted the same. In their five senses, in their sex and emotion, they had achieved a oneness in which their colors blended.

#### #2

It was as if the night had mounted her, as if that was the thing intruding between her slim legs and bringing the first bright pain and then slowly, steadily, rhythmically piercing her. The night, not the man, had the feel of wool and warm flesh and the smell of old cigarettes. She lay open to the night and it came rushing in like the sweet dark burst of life itself, and behind the broad slant of its shoulder the world dropped away and time and the long hurting memories, the dead faces.

Then, slowly, images, long imbedded in her mind, rose and died with each intrusive thrust: that Sunday long ago in Prospect Park—the lovers on the slope, the sense of being free of herself on the ridge above the ball field, then Beryl's secret and her despair . . . Suggie languorous and laughing amid her tumbled sheets . . . the girl proudly whispering of her seduction in the lunchroom . . . it was like being sick and having her father carry her up to the high bed and sinking, feverish, into its soft depth. . . .

From Brooklyn we move to Jamaica:

#### #3

Mark was still bent on getting Jean to give up her virginity, though he kept telling her that he could wait. Meanwhile, she discovered self-pleasing ways of satisfying him. Meanwhile, she wondered whether she was still technically a virgin; there was no part of his body or hers that they had not explored together. She did not like to admit it to herself, but Monica was right about the risk of falling in love with a man's body: She was in danger of idolizing Mark's penis. It became an object of endless fascination — its unfailing response to the merest brush of her hands, first the slight movement and hardening under his pants, then the rigidity; the way its owner would stop everything and surrender to her. She pondered the pros and cons of letting him do what he yearned to do. He had promised that he would not get her pregnant, and anyway she knew how to take precautions. It was not that. From all she had seen and heard, she surmised that sex was a high-risk game in which there was always a winner and a loser. So far, she seemed to be winning. He longed for her. He did everything he could to drive her crazy with desire, to cause her to lose control and yield to him — which she never did. It would have amazed Monica to learn how far, in this regard, Jean was able to out-Monica her.

And memories of Africa:

### #4

Now I remember when my father died, but not how. It was beautiful. All the women went to the chatree hut in the middle of our village and danced all night. There men usually stayed, smoking, wrapping wounds, picking chigoes from their feet, feeding the fire, arguing, sometimes fighting over the last mouthful of changa-wine left in the pan. But tonight only women, naked, painting each other's breasts and bellies with the resemblances of animals, and howling in mirth, and drinking as greedily as men would, and banging their fists upon the earth, and only I am pemitted to be among them, all the men and child-folk banished to their huts. My mother too. She is in our garden, watching over my father who is wrapped in breta-bark, which yields a soft powdery incense. Her eyes witness him; as candles rage against the gloom and stillness of an English chapel.

In this whirl and canvas of dye I move. A jungle of breasts is offered me, for tonight, only tonight, my father dead, all the women are my wives, by antique custom. I can choose to hunt the young gazelle or the red-lipped snake. The women stamp their feet around me, and drink and drink. They shudder and fall to the ground, pretending to be slain beasts. They offer me a knife to skin them; to rip from their bellies my patrimony; which are pictures of my fathers' lust; the young gazelle, the red-lipped snake.

Now I remember, and have new words to remember, how beautiful it was, the chorus and the exhibition of shameless painted women. I am brought into manhood—even as an extreme child—by the play of their nipples; and their bodies conjure forth the heat from my blood; till I grow numb, anointed in cold glues which flow from their nakedness, and breath leaves my mouth in troubling song and I become the father whom my mother tends, her ears bent to his dead lips; listening for any trace of sound, any canticle of the love which once hardened within her, scraping and paining like a sackful of ebo-flints, forming the child which gave birth to me.

To the beach for our final quiz passage:

#5

They lay side by side, naked, the tall handsome black boy and the statuesquely beautiful black girl. The song of the surf was the only sound in the moonlit world. And because they were on a private fenced-in beach they lay relaxed, unafraid of intruders or the night prowlers who preyed on lovers on lonely beaches. Besides, they were an hour's drive out of the city and the night prowlers operated at public beaches much nearer to the city.

The boy was mute with wonder because of the unexpectedness of it all. It had not been what he had intended. They had been here, on this beach, many times in the past, and nothing happened. But unexpectedly, surprisingly and in a manner that he could not now recall, he had made love to her and discovered, with awed dismay, that it was the first time for her. She had taken him in quietly, as a mother suckling a baby at her breast and finding fulfillment in the very hurt of the act. He thought she had wept a little but he could not be sure of anything except that it had been the first time for her and the strange feelings of guilt and wonder this fact had evoked. You would not believe it, with the vast army of admirers always around her, with the whirl of parties and dances she attended, and especially after you'd experienced the competence with which she necked and petted and the casual assurance with which she had joined in any discussion of sex when it arose.

Afterwards they had gone into the warm sea then they had lain on the beach for a long time, her left hand in his right, and he had found himself bereft of speech, like a man struck dumb.

The answers:

#1—Chester Himes

#2—Paule Marshall

#3—Margaret Cezair-Thompson

#4—David Dabydeen

#5—Peter Abrahams

Enjoy the collection.

◄ JENOYNE ADAMS ►

# Resurrecting Mingus

*Jenonye Adams is a fiction writer, poet, and dancer. Her work has been featured in programs at the National Black Arts Festival, Pan African Film Festival, Los Angeles County Museum of Art, and J. Paul Getty Museum. She was born in San Bernardino, California, and currently lives in L.A. with her husband, writer Michael Datcher.*

MINGUS FACED THE TABLE AND UNTIED THE ROBE SLOWLY. Laying face down, she couldn't see Eric but she could hear him rubbing the oil briskly between his hands. When he touched her the first time, her body went into shock. Warm, oily hands enveloped her shoulders. She could feel all his fingers kneading into her flesh.

"Your shoulders are tight," he said, concentrating on a knot in her right shoulder.

"I think that's where I store tension."

"Try stretching a few times a week."

"Yeah," Mingus said, paying more attention to his hands than his words. "Right there."

"This is tense too," he said, massaging her lumbar region.

"You should probably get a massage once a week, at least till the bugs are worked out. Your muscles need to get used to being relaxed."

"I agree," she mumbled to him, while thinking to herself she'd fucked up. Lord, please let this man be who I think he is, she prayed.

His fingers journeyed down her lower back to her behind. Her gluts rolled like dough under his fingers.

"Try not to tense up," he said.

His hands worked her thighs and down to the soles of her feet.

"Okay, turn over."

She turned onto her back and noticed that her nipples were hard. She looked at him to see if he noticed, but his expression was business as usual.

"Would you like a towel to cover your chest until I get to it?"

"No," Mingus said.

He pushed his fingers into the spaces between her toes and wiggled them into submission. After massaging her calves, she watched him squeeze more Emu oil into his hands. He pressed her lower thigh. Chills ran through her body. His fingers inched upward, parting her legs a little with each movement. Her breaths got short and heavy as he kneaded the inner flesh. She braced her hands on either side of the table and tried not to squirm. Eric rolled the lace panties an inch into her hairline. Mingus closed her eyes. With four fingers he massaged her pelvic muscles. Her bottom lip quivered. She held her breath. Eric moved up both sides of her stomach to the outside of her breasts. In small circular motions his fingers mowed inward toward her nipples until they swelled with color in his hands.

"Ahh." Mingus's body started to squirm. "Eric, ahh."

His hands plunged deeper into her breast.

"Please," she said.

His fingers moved to her neck. Her body twisted and turned like a thousand kneading hands swarming her body.

He stood above her head and leaned in close.

"The neck should never be handled roughly," he said.

Mingus watched the sexy groove of his lips as he talked—how his tongue slid across pink-purple flesh leaving a trail of moistness behind.

Eric finished her neck with feather soft caresses and took Mingus's hand. She followed him upstairs, past two closed doors into his bedroom. The carpet rose and fell under her feet. Eric let go of her hand and bent down a few feet in front of her, lighting the fireplace with a long wooden match. Mingus stood still, watching the movement of the flame. Still on his knees, he pulled his sweatshirt over his head. The orange shadows hugged his curly-haired chest. Shit, Mingus thought. He pulled her into him like he had in her living room. They stood on their knees, bare chests touching.

BENDING her head into his lap, he slid his open palm down her back. The roll of her skin between his fingers caused a rippling under the surface, each wave more intense than the one before.

25

Eric held the back of her neck in his left hand and with his right, pulled two pins from her hair. "It's over," Mingus said into his lap, all resistance gone from her body. He massaged her scalp with strong hands. His skin met the fire at her roots. He was burrowing into a private place. A place where the right man's comforts could sooth away distrust and bad endings. A place where she loved like the first time. A place where she wanted to be touched.

"Eric," she gasped, shaking her head.

"Relax, baby."

All she could do was breathe.

He laid her on her back and looked down at her as he unbuttoned his jeans. The first button popped from its slit. His legs were thick; his ass a sprinter's—firm, wide, tight, and black.

"I can't take this."

No response. No smile. He stared her in the eye like he was meaning business. Kneeling between her ankles, he raised her foot to his mouth. He licked up her calf and bit the tendon above her heel. Mingus grabbed for his chest. He dodged his bald head into her pubic hair and careened it about until her legs spread into eagle wings and she was holding his ears, pumping to his rhythm. Mothafucka. Mingus vowed right then and there—only a bald man belonged between her legs.

Mingus's back tensed into an arch, her fingers suctioned to the back of his head. He snatched her hands away and stretched them high above her head, holding her crisscrossed wrists with one hand. With the other, he reached under the bed. His body covered her like a second skin. He placed a black-and-gold square between his teeth and ripped it open. Mingus closed her eyes. Anticipation caused her to gyrate as his hip forced her legs to open wider. She had never been so wet. As he worked into his groove, he placed his hands in hers and began to rise and fall on top of her like a heavy blanket making smoke signals over fire.

He rode faster and faster, then slowed his entire body to a halt except for his penis that pulsed small vibrations through her tightening pelvis.

"I can't take this," she said shutting her eyes, "it's too much."

Eric grabbed the sides of her face almost gently.

"Look at me. You can take this. Let your body relax. Trust me. I got you."

Mingus softened her apprehensions and let her body be enveloped.

"Right there, baby?"

"Yes," she whispered into his neck.

"Work it, Ming. Yeah, you got it baby. Awh yeah." He rode faster and faster. "You gonna make me come. Work it, Ming."

Ming. She hadn't been called that in a long time. Her dad used to call her that when she was little. Eva used to tease her about it, "Daddy's Ming," she would say with contention in her eyes.

Eric kissed her stomach and rolled onto the rug. He nudged her onto his chest. She maneuvered her head under his chin. He smoothed her hair out of his face.

"You want to go home tonight?" he said.

"No."

Eric hugged her tighter. "Did you come?"

"Yeah, what about you?"

"You know I did. You were working and wiggling."

Eric gyrated, pretending to be her.

"Be quiet. You tried to work me to death."

"Bed is no place to be holding back."

"I'll remember that next time."

◀️ ASHA BANDELE ▶️

# The Prisoner's Wife

*Asha Bandele has written one collection of poetry,* Absence in the Palms of My Hands, *and* The Prisoner's Wife, *the love story between a beautiful, talented college student and a man serving twenty to life for murder. She writes for* Honey *magazine and lives in Brooklyn, New York.*

MY BODY USED TO TRY TO KILL ME EVERY TIME I PARTED MY LIPS or my legs, willingly or unwilling. It would choke me in this crazy undercover way that no one else ever noticed, but for me there was no air. Even during the rare occasions that someone actually loved me, when my lover would take his time with me, remember the color of my eyes, even then the passageway to my lungs would sputter and finally lock itself tight into itself. My own body choked me from the inside out, letting me live only for the pleasure of its next attack. It was some wild shit.

And so that evening my eyes studying first my hard brown nipples and approving of them; my eyes moving down and accepting, if not fully satisfied with, my round though not fat stomach; and my stomach with its light-colored stretchmarks and fine line of black hair that begins at my navel and follows a straight line down to my pussy; that evening taking all of this in, taking all of this me in without cringing or critiquing, was indeed progress.

In our four years together, I had come to believe, Rashid had helped me come to believe, that even my stomach is sexy, that I am sexy. It was the way he would become transfixed on some part of me. From my eyes to my ass, he always told me, in blushing detail, how beautiful I was.

*Don't no man want to feel no rock up under him, Asha,* he said to me during the trailer visit as we stood in front of a mirror looking at ourselves, examining who together we appeared to be.

*Girl, you're the way a woman supposed to be, sweet and thick. You nobody's fat so get that shit out your head. You just don't look like them sick-ass white girls from those magazines. And you not supposed to look like that. Shoot. I want a real woman. I want a Black woman. I want a fine woman. And that's what I got.*

That first visit Rashid had forced me to look at myself, nude, in the mirror, with all the lights on.

*Look at yourself, Momi,* Rashid had said. *You so god-damn beautiful!*

I had looked because he had made me look, but I felt my pupils try to curl shut. I squinted and strained, to see through myself, to see only the glass of the mirror, but it didn't work. I wanted to see my body as an indistinguishable brown mass, but Rashid refused me my selective blindness.

I watched as he smoothed his hands up my thighs, up my

stomach, cupping my breasts from behind. He had run his tongue over his fingertips, and now they played with my nipples, which brought out in me an involuntary moan and then scream, arch and then grind. After all of our years of talking, all of our fantasies poured out to each other, slowly, through whispers or giggles, after all the visits when we talked because we could not touch, he knew me, and he knew that he knew me.

He knew my body, its fears, and its every nerve and yearning. He knew how my face looked when the hunger became too strong to be contained. He knew everything I had ever told him, everything I had never told him, everything I had never even thought about myself. He knew at that moment I was so desperately wet that he could have felt it down the inside of my legs if he wanted to. And he wanted to, but he waited.

He made us both wait as he smiled slightly, noticing the way my tongue and teeth played with my lips, how they reached for something to hold, to suckle, to swallow. I am telling you, I needed that man to fill me everyway and everywhere.

Have you ever loved like that, where there is no part of your lover you do not want to be touched and, finally, filled by? That's how I wanted him, in every opening I had.

Rashid kissed the back of my neck, bit the back of my neck, and whispered,

*What you want, girl?*

*P-P-lease* . . . I managed. *P-P-lease* . . . I managed again, fearful he didn't hear me the first time.

With one hand on my back he eased me down until I was

31

bent all the way over. My hands balanced me on the floor, his hands steadied him against my hips.

He slipped inside me naturally, with no struggle, no searching. Inside me he was tight, fitted and perfect, and I felt certain, with each sweet, long stroke he made, that I was made, like some cherished encasing, just for him.

And my lungs, they just expanded as I breathed him, as I breathed him and I breathed me, into every one of my open and wanting pores.

❧ AKOSUA BUSIA ☙

# The Seasons of
# Beento Blackbird

*Akosua Busia was born in Ghana, educated in Europe, and cur-
rently lives in Los Angeles. As an actress, she appeared with
Whoopi Goldberg in* The Color Purple. *As a novelist, she is currently working on her second book. This excerpt is from* The Seasons of Beento Blackbird, *her debut novel.*

MIRIAM LAY ON THE BED IN THE MOONGLOW, NAKED BETWEEN
the thin white sheets, freshly bathed and scented, with her thick,
black, curly hair threaded out across the white lace pillow, like al-
gae on a lake of water lilies. Solomon stood by the door, laughter-
tickled raindrops dripping down his body onto the floor. He slid
his eyes along the contours of Miriam's form, feasting himself on
her shapeliness. Inspired by her curves, he peeled off his rain-
soaked shirt and stepped up to the bed.

Clutching the sheet, Miriam rose to her knees, touched her
palm against his smooth wet chest. Her soft lips a whisper away
from his own, he could feel her warm breath blowing across
the ridge of his mouth. "Behold King Solomon in all his

glory," she praised, spreading her fingers open across his chest like a fan.

Solomon shuddered at the tenderness of her touch. A thrill of excitement rippled through his body as it responded to the attention of her stroking hand. "Beautiful," Miriam moaned as she trailed her fingers across his chest, off his flesh, and lay back down on the bed. "Beautiful, beautiful King Solomon."

Solomon looked down at Miriam sprawled before him on the bed. There she was, rib of his rib. He had traveled the world over, and no one had those sensuous heavy lids half-masted over hazy hazel eyes, surrounded by those lashes that curled and reached for attention. Or that gypsy-wild black hair, framing those high cheekbones. Or that wide inviting mouth that could hold you prisoner in its smile. He peeled away the top sheet, revealing her creamed-coffee curves that beckoned him come. Easing his eyes over her naked body, he ran the top of his middle finger slowly down her forehead, her nose, her lips, her neck, through the center of her collarbone, stroked it between her heavy breasts, tickle-traced it down into the dip of her belly button—Miriam gasped, held her breath as he wiggled the top of his finger in the little hollow, then rotated it in tiny circles, around and around, wider and wider, over the smooth curve of her stomach, down into her thick curly hairs. She gasped again, letting out the faintest trace of a moan. Solomon smiled, unbuckled his belt, and stripped naked.

# Your Blues Ain't Like Mine

*Bebe Moore Campbell is the recipient of a National Endowment for the Arts Literature Grant as well as a National Association of Negro Business and Professional Women's Literature Award. Her first novel,* Your Blues Ain't Like Mine *(from which this excerpt is taken) won an NAACP Image Award. Her other works include* Brothers and Sisters, Singing in the Comeback Choir, *and* What You Owe Me. *She lives in Los Angeles.*

THE MUSIC WAS AS MUCH A GIFT AS SUNSHINE, AS RAIN, AS ANY blessing ever prayed for.

Lily woke up when the singing began. She lay quiet and still in her bed until her head was full of songs and the strong voices of the fieldworkers from the Pinochet Plantation seemed to be inside her. Part of the song was soft like a hymn; then it would rise to the full force of vibrant gospel and change again to something loud and searing, almost violent. The music was rich, like the alluvial soil that nourished everything and everyone in the Delta. Lily began to feel strong and hopeful, as if she was being healed. Colored people's singing always made her feel so good.

Much too quickly, the song was over, without even leaving an echo to keep her company. Years later, she would fight to hum even a scrap of the notes that floated to her from the Pinochet Plantation that day, but by then the song had seeped into the land like spilled blood, and its vanishing echo was just another shadow on her soul.

As Lily lay in bed looking out the window into the wee hours of that Mississippi morning, it seemed as if someone had drawn down a heavy black curtain on the world. She felt lonely and adrift in the sudden quiet. Daylight was at least an hour away, and she couldn't fall back asleep. She groped in the dark toward the still body of her husband, who was lying next to her.

With movements as quick and furtive as a thief's, Lily pressed her breasts into Floyd's bare back; she wanted him to wake up feeling the tips of her nipples against his skin, the slight undulating movement of her groin rotating against his behind. It was like the ticking of a clock, the way her crotch burrowed into him: a small relentless movement. He'd been gone for nearly ten days and had returned earlier that evening. She felt frightened and weak when he was away from her. It was as though she didn't exist when he was absent. As she pressed into him, rubbing his shoulder blades with the tips of her nipples, she thought of how excited he would be when he woke up. She smiled, thinking how she could make him want her, remembering the times he even begged. Maybe he would plead with her this time. She might yawn a little and act uninterested, which would only make him hotter. She gently stroked his behind with her thigh, over and over again. Lily squeezed her small, white body against Floyd's back and rested the side of her face on his shoulder blade. She kissed his spine and thought: *If I can get him to give me three dollars, I'll get me another Rio Red lipstick; ain't had a lipstick in going on three months. I might can buy me some Evening in Paris and a scarf too. And maybe some rose-colored nail polish.* The thought of the lipstick, the bottle of perfume, the scarf, and the nail polish made her breath come heavy and fast. She calmed herself, because the trick was to wake Floyd softly, to let him discover her squeezed against him, to make it seem coincidental that the front of her nightgown was undone, her breasts exposed. Wanting her had to be his idea; he didn't like it the other way around. Floyd said only whores acted that way.

Looking out the window, Lily could see that a soft, drizzling mist was coming down. It had rained almost the entire time that Floyd had been gone, a hard, driving rain that rattled the tin roof and leaked into the pots and pans she placed strategically throughout the house. Not that it made a dent in the September heat spell they'd been seeing in Mississippi, Lily thought. Probably just fatten up the old mosquitoes and breed new ones. She wondered if her husband would ever fix the roof.

Lily's body was soft and slightly damp, like the weather. She could smell the musty odor coming from between her legs and clamped her thighs shut to keep the scent away from Floyd. When they put in a bathroom, she would take baths every night. Bubble baths. Beneath the thin sheet, she could feel her husband's first waking movements. She wrapped her arm around his waist and squeezed his belly, thinking as she breathed softly into the nape of her husband's neck—which was speckled with dirt he hadn't bothered to wash off—about the $67.58 in his pants pocket, pay for a week of construction work in Louisiana. Then, just seconds before he woke up, she fell away from him, so that only her nipples grazed his back. It was easy to let her mouth fall open, to push a soft, sleepy moan from her lips. She thought: *I can make him do what I want now.*

Lily opened her eyes slowly when he touched her. Fully awake, they admired each other. They were beautiful in similar ways; the people in the town used to mistake them for brother and sister. They both had glossy, dark curls, the same full lips and bright green eyes. They were a pair, all right. Lots of folks told them that they were the best-looking couple in the Delta.

"You are a pretty thing," Floyd said. He put his hands on Lily's breasts, then wriggled down in the bed and began sucking one of her nipples, gently at first and then with growing force. He pushed her gown up, then grabbed her hips, pulling her into his groin; he put his fingers between her legs and pushed up inside her, Lily felt a sudden fire there. She wanted to cry out, "Harder!"—she often wondered what the harm in that would be—but she said nothing. As Lily closed her eyes, bright colors swirled around her head. She could feel herself opening up in sweet anticipation.

Floyd slid into her too fast, then began rocking and pumping and pressing, his fingers grabbing and kneading all the wrong places. Lily opened her eyes. Disappointment gripped her shoulders like an old friend. She wanted to cry out, to tell him to stop, that nothing he was doing felt good, but she kept quiet, realizing that her power was gone, that she would have to ride out the storm. Go numb.

She had learned to do that years before.

She bit down on her lip and threw her arms around Floyd and held on as tightly as she could until she felt his shudders and hard spasms; then she closed her eyes and let out a practiced moan. When her last sigh faded, she fell away from him with relief.

# Don't the Moon Look Lonesome: A Novel in Blues and Swing

*Stanley Crouch is the author of* Always in Pursuit, The All-American Skin Game *(nominated for a National Book Critics Circle Award), and* Notes of a Hanging Judge. *He is an editorial columnist for the* New York Daily News, *artistic consultant to Jazz at Lincoln Center, and the recipient of a MacArthur fellowship. This selection is from his first novel,* Don't the Moon Look Lonesome: A Novel in Blues and Swing.

HE STOOD AND PUT HIS HANDS IN HER DAMP HAIR, WHICH HAD—IF you asked her—no character but *felt*, even in its flatness, as though each strand of her whole story was growing from her skull into his fingers when the mood was like this. Such was the Midas touch that led to softening a woman, not hardening her. That's what it was. It let Carla possess every drop of the swampy goo inside her own soul. She was all steam and boiling sugar. She knew it then because she couldn't breathe and she couldn't stop breathing. There was also no better feeling in the universe than the way his warm hand would rub her wet back so gracefully as he turned her around to unsnap the moist brassiere. Standing now in her panties only, which Maxwell always made a production of removing once they got to the bed, she loved taking off his shirt, kissing the back of his neck, repeatedly but carefully nipping his shoulders, then unbuckling his belt and experiencing the scintillation that came as her thumb and forefinger pulled the zipper down slowly so that each metal tooth had its say in the night air.

They then met in the place where men and women meet, the place they both have to arrive in, her one way, him another, both bringing the syllables of feeling necessary to create the rhyme of all time. That was what her man jokingly referred to when he called either from somewhere in the city or out on the road. There was no greeting when she answered, just a pause. Then it began. He asked, his voice low and soft, almost like that of an aroused stranger. Sometimes he was inventing a way into something close to mischief, what Carla considered a cute brand of teasing:

"Say, is this here the palace of the crown princess of the posteriototti?"

"It could be."

"Hey, baby, how's the fuzzy-wuzzy school of South Dakota Kama Sutra moves?"

"Just what, exactly, are you referring to, sir?"

"Viking Hottentot. Serious business."

"As in?"

"That's what I'm talking about—as *in*. How is that blonde Hottentot institution? I'm talking about that rump roast, which also offers hot velvet courses in marine polyrhythms."

"Excuse me. Excuse me! Have you got the correct phone number?"

"How is that finishing school for high-class boudoir action doing—right about now?"

"Oh, *that*. Well, well. What can I say? Let me see. It's doing all right. There."

"You think you can still be sweet enough to get your heart *all* the way down there?"

"You got to bring a heart to meet a heart, big boy. Mine will be right there waiting. In the Kama Sutra steam room, where the fish smell fresh and clean. Just for you. Sweetheart."

There was then a pause and some contemplative breathing she found exciting.

"Carla, baby, aw, *baby!* Whew. Now *that's* exactly why I love you, baby. *Exactly* why."

"Come on home, honey boy. Come on home to me, daddy. I'm so hot I can't stand it. I want to feel that thrill when I hear your feet on the steps and the key turn in the lock. I want the touch of your lips, Maxwell. I want us to make love to each other until we turn into two balls of fire."


WELL, now *that* was over. No more playing around and having silly, cutesy-poo pornographic conversations that would have embarrassed the both of them out of New York if anybody else had ever heard them. How long had it been since he talked with her like that, or she had listened to herself saying things to him nothing out of the past foreshadowed at all? He was different this last year and didn't care to sneak behind her in the shower, his shirt, pants, and shoes on, saying he just couldn't wait to be against her skin, which made him seem so foolish and childish but so much *her* man as the two of them removed his clothes until he stood before the girl from South Dakota in all the rippling bulk of his masculinity, washing and turning her and whispering her name, the two of them so free of everything but each other.

There were no more times when his eloquence startled her as she lay on her round stomach in the sensually itching blackness of the night and he told his baby how beautiful her form was to his hands, that the rise between her waist and the top of her thighs was a full hill of romantic dignity, that the down on the back of her neck was a beard of sunlight, that she was perfect because each nuance of honeysuckle tenderness was equaled by a spear of smokeless fire that made lying against her feel like he was moving across the top of a sugar cake covered with lit candles that didn't burn but gave him fresh, impeccably luscious sensations, that the two of them making love was another kind of talk, a conversation in which the flesh and the words of love and the wordless noises of love summed up what Ellington meant when he said that a man and a woman going steady were the world's greatest duet.

That wasn't all. Not with Maxwell. In the afterglow, there were experiences that touched Carla so wholly she might find herself transported close to a sob by the sentiment in his body. She and her man would lie there together, wet and salty from all the action, and he would embrace his deliciously exhausted baby, hugging her as though his heart had become his arms. The succession of hugs were of different pressures, slight to powerful but never even close to hurting her, only one statement after another of emotion beyond even the realm of whispers, emotion so clear in those embraces that her own insides became more evident to Carla as they tingled, bells of fresh feeling going off at the prompting of those increasingly expressive hugs that misted her up. Maxwell would then delicately move his hands across her back, her thighs, her bottom, her calves, her shoulders, her waist, the half-moon crest of her belly, her forehead, her temples, her cheeks, and her neck, made to seem so much longer by the quality of the way he put his fingers to each inch of it. All of these subtle things for maybe an hour, kissing her here and there so, so softly and somehow coaxing both of their bodies to relax, from the forehead to the feet, until the skin of each one became porous enough for even more feeling to breathe itself back and forth, his to hers, hers to his, the slightest touch both an unscented perfume of spirit and an entire tale of passion in gradation upon gradation. She quivered against him then and her heart stood still and sometimes she couldn't stop crying.

Carla needed no help to understand that whenever that happened, the weeping in his arms, it meant that she was in yet another depth of nakedness, responding to the satisfaction of hungers for the unrelenting strokes of romance, hungers their love revealed to her when the intensity of the joy was that gentle. There were still pleasures, yes, but not those, and those leisurely times were the elite moments of recognition that made the arguments as well as the periodic, self-involved moodiness expected of two artists define themselves as nothing but difficult intermissions. It no longer seemed like old times. Romance was a vacation from the way they were living now, not the essence that they always returned to, sometimes full of apologies but always more aware of what had put them so firmly inside of each other. She didn't like the long death of it but faced the truth that the tone of surrender was gaining power in her heart.

# A Harlot's Progress

*David Dabydeen was born in Guyana. He read English at Cambridge and currently teaches at the University of Warwick. He has published three books of poems and four novels, which have won numerous awards. This passage is from* A Harlot's Progress, *his most intellectually complex work to date, a marvelous reworking of Hogarth that's narrated by London's oldest living black inhabitant.*

IN HER FINAL DAYS I TOOK ADVANTAGE OF HER WEAKNESS BY throwing off her blanket and lifting her bodily to the tub to be bathed. She gasped when she set eyes on me, for I was a patchwork of green like areas of the desert Rima and I would scour for food, after the rains conjured forth miraculous blooms. She gazed at the strange green landscape of me with such intensity that I was moved to look upon myself. For the first time I marvelled at strange growths my skin nurtured. Skin that was the curse of my race, bringing slavery upon us, was now a harvest so plentiful that even my planter-father would have been astonished at me. And when I looked upon her I too was dumbfounded by her appearance. I had expected to lift the blanket to a sight piteous beyond words, but was faced instead by unblemished form. Her disease, though it raged violently within her, could not break through to the surface of her. She was the very image of the Virgin depicted in many of Lord Montague's paintings. I lifted her to the tub, and although there was not the least sign of impurity about her, I still bathed her as a means of cleansing myself of the desire I felt for her. My hands explored all the nakedness of her. The trials of slavery were insubstantial compared to the temptations suffocating me with their weight. Each time I touched her I cried for the King's Pardon, for Christ the Executioner to stay His pressing of me, but He let me bleed from the shameful parts of me so that I could better understand my sinfulness. It was not the village Elder marking my forehead nor the women of my tribe dancing nakedly for me, nor Captain Thistlewood's missionary acts, which brought me to an understanding of sin. It was the helpless beautiful body of a harlot which, after I had done with it, I lifted out of the tub with remorse as final as that of the apostle as he lifted Christ's corpse from Calvary.

◆ JULIE DASH ◆

# Daughters of the Dust

*Julie Dash grew up in the Queensbridge Housing Projects in New York City. She earned a degree in film production from the City College of New York and an M.F.A. from UCLA. Her movie,* Daughters of the Dust *(which was made with the assistance of a Guggenheim Research Grant), won awards from the American Film Institute, the Black Filmmakers Hall of Fame, and the Coalition of 700 Black Women. Currently she is working on her second novel as well as various film projects.*

AMELIA TURNED IN HIS ARMS AND SEARCHED HIS FACE IN THE moonlight. She could feel his eyes flitting over the angles of her face, sharpened by the darkness. Reaching out, she traced his lips and felt the pleasure and need ripple across his features. She inhaled, drawing in his scent. There was the salty blend of sweat and sea air, an earthy aroma like fresh-turned dirt, and his own essence, surely something Elizabeth would have used for one of her scents. Her skin prickled with anticipation and she leaned forward and pressed her lips to his. He responded tenderly, allowing her to lead him. She pressed closer, cupping his face and holding him to her as she explored his mouth. He tasted of coffee, molasses, and the sweet mint that the folks chewed like gum. She let her hunger and need take over as her hands stroked his head. His heartbeat was so loud that she felt as if she had climbed into his chest. She broke away and looked up at the moon. "It's moon madness, isn't it?"

He shook his head. "Not for me."

She pulled away from him and stood up, his hands steadying her. She began to unbutton the back of her dress. As her fingers fumbled, she heard him stand and his strong hands took over. He stroked her neck and back as he freed the buttons. He helped her pull the dress over her head and chuckled as she flung it into the air and let it float to the bushes down below. As she stood shivering in the cool night, he opened his rough shirt and pulled her to his chest, wrapping the ends around her. She felt his body stir, and a rush of heat enveloped them. He turned with her in his arms and walked her backward to the broad trunk. When she spread her hands against his chest, he cupped her hips and pulled her to him. As he began to unbutton her camisole, she unlaced his pants and eased them down his legs, each stroke causing him to breathe more deeply. She helped him lift one foot, then the other. Pulling her up into his arms, he pressed her against the trunk and she felt the heat from his body. When he came to her, she hungrily sought all of him, his mouth, his arms, his manhood. As he breathed into her mouth and raised her hips, she knew that she had found her safe place.

# Between Lovers

*Eric Jerome Dickey was born in Memphis, Tennessee, and currently lives in Los Angeles. His previous novels include* Liar's Game *(a New York Times bestseller),* Cheaters, Milk in My Coffee, Friends and Lovers, *and* Sister, Sister—*they were all #1 Blackboard bestsellers. This excerpt is from his 2001 novel,* Between Lovers.

IT'S COLD OUTSIDE. VERY COLD, SOME WIND SINGS IN THE TREES. But we stay in the night's chill.

I pat her hand. She holds my finger. Her lips move, and the expression on her face tells me that she's about to say something positive, something very human, but she doesn't give in. For a moment there is a spiritual connection. My energy mixes with her life force. Almost feels like love.

Her lips look soft, and I remember how they felt when they pressed against mine. Not like I thought they would be. Powerful, magnetic, sweet lips. She licks them. I lick mine. Nicole knows that for me, kissing is the ultimate seduction. I think it means the same to Ayanna. One kiss, we exchange energy, become part of each other for eternity, and no matter how hard we wish to go back to ignorance, we can't, because we're no longer strangers. One kiss, we're familiar forever. Again she licks her lips as she stares at my face. Again I do the same.

Our names are called; we both jump a bit. We step inside like children responding to a bell at the end of recess. No, not recess. Like kids who were caught playing doctor in their parents' closet.

Nicole creeps through the dim candlelight, moves with the ease of a cat, her boldness tuned to high, shoeless so she seems shorter, more vulnerable. Our topless dancer waiting for us to sing her a song of approval, her small brown breasts so round and womanlike. She has a very ethereal expression, and her natural beauty dulls my head, intoxicates me with the power of a shot of heated rum. Nicole winks at Ayanna but comes to me first, energetic with breathless excitement. She has created this night.

Nicole kisses me, give me little tastes, little bites, we don't rush, nibbling lips, taking each other's breath until every cell in my body catches fire. She's tipsy, her breath sweet and sour, her flesh so eager. She pulls my head to her right breast, the most sensitive one, my favorite appetizer, and gives her thick nipple to me and I praise it with the warmth and wetness of my mouth, fall into my own music, my own rhythm; the world falls away.

Ayanna is watching us.

Trembles roll through Nicole's body. That excites me.

"Ayanna," Nicole says. "Come here, kiss me, baby."

Ayanna eases into our space, her patchouli aroma mixing with Nicole's herbal scent, and while I feed and caress her wonderful breast, above me are the sounds of tender whines and deep kisses. Their breaths create a warm breeze raking against my neck, flowing into my hair.

Ayanna is swallowing Nicole's throaty moans. She has one hand on Nicole's other breast, the other moving up and down the round of Nicole's butt. My fingers drift between Nicole's legs, fingers raking across her soft, damp, narrow hole, massaging that spot that swells, touching Ayanna's humid fingers at the same time, both of us trying to prove that we can please Nicole better than the other.

All the sounds that Nicole has made for me, all the noise that I wish were special for me, echo for Ayanna as well. Maybe even better, because this is her greatest fantasy, and she responds to the dual stimulation with more intensity.

Nicole inhales hard through her nose, releases air in spurts from her mouth, as if she were sprinting up a steep hill. Her right leg trembles, face furrows with pleasure as she shivers and moans, her words so hot and humid, "Shit, I'm not ready to come. Not yet. Let's take a shower."

Ayanna catches her breath, motions toward the sunken tub next to the shower, says, "I'd rather bathe."

I know what Ayanna's doing, trying to delay. The same reason she diverted us to San Francisco.

"Next time," Nicole says. "We'll eat fruit and bathe together next time."

And that is the end of that.

Nicole is always so very clean. Another thing I've always loved about her, always appreciated about her. Always smells fresh, never musty, never owns any after-pee taste down in the triangle. My Queen of Clean Hygiene doesn't treat us like slaves, but instead becomes our servant, the one who is aiming to please two. She undresses Ayanna, kisses Ayanna's breasts, her neck, her eyes, her fingers, touches her between her legs, does all of that as Ayanna blinks in and out of what she is feeling and watches me. I lick my lips. Somewhere between sweltering breaths, Ayanna does the same, blinks and licks and blinks and licks. My eyes stay on her body, which is slim, not much to behold. But she's toned, she's articulate, she's blunt, she's intelligent, she's feminine, she's athletic, she's arrogant, she's confident, she's aggressive, so I understand what's erotic and appealing about her. We're physical people who thrive on mental stimulation. Fools with educations and ambitions, and attracted to the same.

Ayanna's breasts remind me of sunrise in Maui, and her nipples are blacker than the long winter nights in Alaska. The most beautiful nipples I've ever seen. Full, erect, so thick. Blackberries screaming to be taken into a nice warm mouth. Moisture rises on her skin like morning dew. My eyes drift over her curves, over her lines, drift until they stop on her vagina, on her true ayanna, a beautiful flower with soft, curly black hair.

My adversary and me stare at each other, licking our lips, struggling to remember the rules of this war.

Seeing a woman naked for the first time is like visiting a new place. It forces you to take in the texture, inhale all the sweet smells, crave the tastes, admire a marvelous creation, encourages you to pack up your needs and journey into the unknown.

To become immersed in that land, in its hills and valleys, to wet your mouth in the rivers, to be drawn into the undercurrents.

Nicole removes my pants, underwear, socks, shirt. Folds my clothes and leaves some things on the brown leather chair, some things on the leather ottoman. My skin is cool but nervous sweat trickles down my back, finds its way into the crack of my rear.

Ayanna gazes at the lines that add up to me. No breathless excitement, just confidence and relaxed shoulders, then a long stare with piercing eyes that make me feel as if the skin is gone from my body.

At last, we're all naked in Nicole's garden.

◄{ TREY ELLIS }►

# Platitudes

*Trey Ellis was born in Washington, D.C., in 1962. He was edu-*
*cated at Andover and Stamford, worked in Italy as a translator,*
*and has traveled extensively throughout Central America and*
*Africa. His novels include* Platitudes, Home Repairs, *and* Right
Here, Right Now. *He lives in Santa Monica, California.*

I NEED TO HOLD SOMEBODY, SAYS JANEY, LAYING HER ARM OVER
his shoulder. Her nose strokes his neck, her lips smear his jugu-
lar, her eyelashes brush his jaw. A tear from her touches hot,
lengthens quickly to his collarbone, stops, wells again, lengthens
quickly under his shirt, over his breast to ball over his nipple. He
hugs her, he sweeps his hands over the back of her silk blouse
(*sheepsheepsheep*). She kisses his jaw, his chin, his lips; the tip of
the tongues lightly touch, lightly touch, swirl over each other.
Janey squeezes Earle's chest, then pulls away.

Come on, she says, rising, raising his hand, pulling him up.

She opens the door, and her father's wide bedroom again vi-
brates brown: mahogany and tortoiseshell and smoked glass. Inside she carefully presses closed the door, she pulls loose the bow

around her blouse's neck, she unbuttons it, then dips each shoulder, pulling her arms from the soft holes of silk. She pushes the plaid kilt off her hips, pushes the white slip off her hips, steps from her brown loafers. She reaches behind herself with both hands, unlatches the bra clasp, squeezes her shoulders forward; the bra falls to her elbows, then to the rug. She pushes her white panties off her hips, off her knees; they drop to her toes, she steps free.

She steps toward Earle carefully; his blazer and tie already cover the brown couch. Then he too is nude and she hugs him again, they kiss again. I'm on the pill now. She kisses his dark ear. Both his brown hands replace the white bra, her red nipples grow to warmly stigmatize his palms. He flushes. The sable penis has now risen higher, taps her lily hip. They slow-dance to the bed, kneel together, then lower themselves to the wide support. Rolling on top of him, she rises, her white knees at his colored waist, the vagina at the penis. Earle looks at them, at her creamy breasts, at her face. She smiles. He smiles too. She holds his raven penis, insinuates it into her snowy self. They smile again. Hers is hot and soft; his warm and hard. Her pearl hands pad his inky shoulders; she raises, lowers herself onto, off of him. Her mouth is soon big, her eyes very closed. As her rhythm increases, her thighs flex, relax around him, her white stomach flexes, relaxes too, her wine nipples *are* warm erasers, she *does* moan as he presses her breasts. Cries rise from her mouth but start somewhere much deeper. She now curves back, her fingers squeeze her hair, her elbows high, riding no-handed, cries now short and quick. Then slow.

*MmmmmmmmmmmMmmmmm.* She rises from him, kisses hard his face, her breasts smear on his chest, her hips and thighs jam the penis, so she lies over him crossways, kisses down the curve of his chin and neck to his clavicle, to each breast; kisses down his stomach, kisses through his pubic hair, returns to kiss his navel. She tilts her head, licks at the penis, at the scrotum, especially the intertesticular area, then licks the underside of the darker ring high on the penis's neck, then the cap itself. She breathes full, eclipses his penis with her mouth. She raises and lowers her face over it, now steadying it with the lips while the tongue presses that darker ring. Earle watches the ceiling as he tugs a bit at her arm, her side, her leg, until she has rotated over him, kneeling. His hands braid over the two small dimples low on her back, then he pulls up to the vagina to press with his pink tongue her pink clitoris, which shines.

Straining between licks, each lap makes the other tighten or curve. Then Janey breathes a long and high cry, twitches quickly. Now Earle breathes long and high, he freezes, then twitches and pumps. Eventually she raises her mouth from his penis—a moist and even gasket.

◈ NURUDDIN FARAH ◈

# Secrets

*Nuruddin Farah's novels include* Sweet and Sour Milk, Sardines,
*and* Close Sesame. *His works have been translated into seven-
teen languages. After* Sweet and Sour Milk *was published, Farah
became persona non grata in his native Somalia. In exile, he declared he would, ". . . keep my country alive by writing about it."*
Secrets, *from which this excerpt is taken, is without doubt one of
the great works of modern African literature. Farah lives in Nige-
ria with his wife and children.*

BETWEEN LOVERS: A SECRET TENSION.

This is all the more so if dealing with a fluke of a day in my life
and Nonno's. For I, Sholoongo, on this my fluke day, with all my
faculties functioning at their optimum, do hereby declare that I
slipped into one ancient man's bed, namely Nonno, even if the
bed was actually Kalaman's, it being the one the young man used
when putting up at Grandfather Nonno's estate. If I mention
Kalaman as the putative user of the bed, it is because beds have a
place of juridical importance in Islam when it comes to determin-
ing paternity. Without going off on a tangent, I should like to

quote from Prophet Mohammed's tradition here. In order to disentangle the knots in the blood of a baby under dispute between two claimant fathers, the Prophet passed a landmark judgment in which he said, "The baby is the bed's." I take this to mean that whichever of the two men owned the bed was the child's father. I am no jurist, and far be it from me to suggest that the Prophet or learned Islamists would give a moment's heed to my sinful use of the sacred tradition. But my point, for what it is worth, is that since Nonno and I were in a bed associated for sleeping purposes with his grandson, the baby, if I should bear one, would be the child of Kalaman, not its putative biological parent, namely Nonno.

Something else entered into my calculations when I slipped into Nonno's bed as the ancient man was busy negotiating a difficult bend in a catnap. I was aware that Nonno would think a hundred times before throwing me out of his house, or before rudely turning down my advances. I reckoned he might plead with me, but he would never bring himself to demand point-blank that I "scram out of his sight" as Kalaman might if I dared slip into *his* bed. Nonno was of the old world, his operating principle being that a gentleman, out of deference to tradition, does not lightly earn for himself the wrath of *nabsi*. I was confident as I went about the business of getting into bed with Nonno that I would have my way with him one way or the other. I knew that Kathy had had hers with him, fully conscious of his old-world sensibilities. With *nobsi-wrath* paramount in his assessments, he wouldn't send me off without a fair hearing.

How he rose at my teasing touch! My goodness: what an

erection of singular handsomeness, Nonno's. I wish the world could see what I saw, a sex of stupendous smoothness as if oiled, veined, a well-rooted body of muscles, collagen, and elastic fiber, these expanding up into a mushroom-shaped dome. At my touch, it rose to meet me, hardening with the pressures of excitement, and due also to the blood level rising. What a shame, too, that in this hour of terrible happenings, of men with scorpioid associations being bumped off, and of the entire Nonno lineage in resultant turmoil, I pursue a stain no bigger than a fly, a live active stain, jellylike in its consistency, clear as sunshine at siesta time. I ask for your Spanish pardon as I take the stand and reveal that I am privy to a death. No, I am not an accessory to the committal of the murder. Moreover if you kindly hold your ostriches, nobody has died, not yet. This much I can confirm. But someone will die soon. Anyway!

I was in Nonno's bed, naked. I sat up, the sheet covering the old man's body, save his sex, which I kept teasing, whose opening I touched again and again in an up and down motion. Why he was in Kalaman's bed I couldn't tell. Maybe he had wet his bed, as some men in their second or third childhoods do, on account of their prostate condition. Myself, I enjoyed the sense of privacy Nonno's estate afforded me: a room for him, many others for guests. I was thinking how people like Nonno have a set of arrangements of the musical-chair sort, Kalaman sleeping in a bed of his, Nonno's, and the old man taking his siesta in his grandson's. This was luxury galore, something a handful of Somalis had at their disposal.

Nonno now awoke with the slowness of a tortoise bringing its head out into view. It struck me that he had no idea where he might be, who I was, or what was happening to him. He might have been dreaming all this up, conjuring into existence a Sholoongo doing the *daba-gur*. Stories abound in Somalia of men performing the *daba-gur* on women, men who, with the woman asleep, insinuate themselves into her bed. The term suggests a gathering of the sleeping woman's robe, and of gradually making an entry from behind, without her consent. Fearful that were she to scream foul she might be condemned for leading the man on, many a woman will submit to this rape of the simulated sort. Damned if they shout for help, and damned and raped if they remain quiet. In such a bind, few of the women on whom the *daba-gur* is practiced succeed in shooing the rapist away.

Of course, mine wasn't a *daba-gur*, for I wasn't approaching Nonno from behind but from the front. It would be *hor-gur*, only I have to coin the term myself, given that no such concept exists in Somali, even though we know it happens. Talk of being unfair to women! I can assure you that even if there was no word to describe what I, a woman, was doing to Nonno, a man, the fact is that the perpetrator of the act and the victim are both supposed to dwell in a world of pretend, both supposed to participate in a simulation. The woman, to bring it to an end, fusses, threatening to cry for help. The man, to bring it to fruition, employs all kinds of tactics, including promising to marry. But we did no such thing, Nonno and I.

When he came to and realized what was afoot, he complained

of the fog in his vision, at a stroke affecting a feeling of helplessness. Falling for his deflective strategy, I requested that he tell me what was ailing his eyes. He explained that, because of a hurt in his eyes, he felt as though his vision had been halved. Now, I had never known anyone suffering from a sudden partial eclipse of vision. I inquired what, in his view, might have caused it. Not enlightening me, he was as elusive as ever, speaking in riddles. He said, "An eternity is anathema by another name."

My hand was by my side. He was flaccid.

"How do you mean?" I said.

"I am a candle burning at both ends," he said, "and which is extinguished by the blowing breeze working directly upon it, under direct orders from other natural phenomena operating within its vicinity. My vision is a candle put out by a forefinger coming into contact with a thumb!"

He was in command. I was spellbound, listening to him. He talked about death, his own and my father's. He alluded to a she-donkey kicking the life out of a man who had stooped to do the *daba-gur* on her. He referred to Fidow's two-way traffic, one carriageway leading him to men, the other to women. Now flaccid, there was something unattractive about him. Even if unaroused, he was big, capable of filling my cupped hands with it. No matter what I did, he refused to rise to my coaxing fingers.

I was set ablaze with vertiginous lust. I was wet down below, eager to be penetrated. Now I was no longer certain of my physical status, my body saying one thing, the mind disapproving. I suppose I saw more of a variety of men and women in my thirty-odd years of life than most, saw a number of them in various degrees of undress. However, I have yet to meet manhoods as exquisite-looking as Nonno's, or for that matter Yaqut's; or a body with as many outlets as Damac's; nor have I run into a man endowed with a belly button as deep as Kalaman's. I know what I'm saying. For I've been the alumna of the three men, even if not Damac's, whom I never got to know in that way.

Lovemaking, at its premium, places demands on the bodily mechanisms of the participants. Nonno was an inactive nonpar-ticipant, half rising at my coaxing but going flaccid as soon as I relaxed. Something was saddening me, though: that I might have been eavesdropping on Nonno's death throes, that I was the last person to see him alive, the last person to give joy to his partially impaired vision. At one point I sensed his physicalness disintegrating right before my very eyes, like milk going bad, the white particles parting with the watery bits, the milk look-alikes undecidedly going hither and thither. No matter.

Now I recalled surprising him one morning before sunrise. This would have been a little over two decades ago. I grabbed him by his sex. My jaws hurt at the memory, at the ferocity of his kick, more hard-hitting than a donkey in heat. As I said, no mat-ter! Because that was years ago. Today I would see to it that I got what I was after.

*Only* I had to pursue him with the same predatory tendencies which, in the end, helped me persuade Kalaman to take thim-blefuls of my feminine trust. Not speaking, the rhythm of his breathing had undergone a substantial change. I touched him.

He rose abundantly, his eyes still shut. He was as immense as a mountain rising out the mist from the beyond, his sex sculpted to please this beholder's eyes.

His mouth opened and shut in the manner of a bull chewing the dusky dream of the day's cud. The man might have been having a wet dream. As I lifted my hind up, prepared to put him inside of me, he shifted his position slightly to the left, clearly in an effort to help. I thought that the *hor-gur* was working. He was letting me have my way. Compatriots of the land of pretend, we were also citizens of the world of stocktaking.

He came. So did I. Tired, breathing heavily, his features collapsed as though they had been constructed out of logs of wood which a great fire had eaten into. The suddenness of it all. I imagined if he had opened his eyes, I might have seen the steel in his gentlemanly resolve, obvious that his mind was in control of his body, able to make it do what he pleased. No trouble at all. I lay prostrate where I was. In a little while I was poised right above him, a vulture ready to perch or fly off in self-preservation. Mine was a predator's greed, success crowning it the first time. Would he give me a second chance? What would I become, a second-time *hor-gur* rapist? What the hell! His sex flaccid, no amount of coaxing or cajoling getting him up, I told myself that he had gone limp on me out of spite. What a bore!

With his back to me in a way that afforded him partial vision of me (a quarter vision, considering the circumstances) I put him whole in my mouth. Soon enough, Nonno was in his distended state. What the heck, I was a bad loser. To turn the tables, I did something to prick his gentleman's conscience. I took him out of my mouth, then started to masturbate right there and then, my forefinger actively going to and fro in rhythmic concause with my moans and groans, the self-fingering crescendo of my defiance increasing in volume louder and louder until he couldn't stand the sad sight and the unbearableness of a young woman drawing sexual pleasure from nothing better than her own forefinger. I told you he was a gentleman. Why, soon after, we were making love.

# E. LYNN HARRIS

# Abide with Me

*Novelist E. Lynn Harris's works include* Invisible Life, Just As I Am, And This Too Shall Pass, *and* If This World Were Mine *(the latter two New York Times bestsellers). In 1996,* Just As I Am *was awarded the Novel of the Year Prize by Blackboard African-American Bestsellers, Inc. The following year,* If This World Were Mine *was nominated for the NAACP Image Award and won the James Baldwin Award for Literary Excellence. This is from his most recent novel.*

BY THE TIME THE ELEVATOR REACHED THE NINTH FLOOR, NICOLE had dabbed an expensive scent behind her ears and on her wrists. She tightened the sash on her coat and slipped her stockingless feet out of her three-inch-high heels.

She followed the plushly carpeted corridor to room 906. Arriving at the room, she set her bag down beside her and placed her shoes on top. As she raised her hand to the door, her heart was pounding and her body throbbed in all the right zones. She took a deep breath and knocked once on the door.

"Who is it?" Jared asked, opening the door a crack.

"It's me," Nicole whispered, "the right woman."

"Prove it," Jared said, opening the door full, but barring her entry into the room with his muscular arms.

The sight of Jared's glistening body, covered only at the waist by a soft blue towel, sent a shivering thrill through Nicole.

"Let me in and I'll give you all the proof you need."

A young couple holding hands passed behind Nicole and giggled as they caught a glimpse of Jared in the doorway.

"I'm sorry, but you'll have to show me your credentials first."

Nicole looked anxiously to her right and to her left. The couple had disappeared around the corner and no one else was in the corridor. She loosened the sash and pulled her coat open and back, letting it slide off her shoulders to the carpet.

Jared took in every inch of Nicole's firm, curvaceous body. Her erect nipples pressed invitingly against the lace of her champagne-colored bra, and her long, smooth showgirl legs extended from the daintiest matching panties.

"Oh, yes," Jared said, "you are most definitely the right woman." He took Nicole's hand and led her into the room. He brought her coat, shoes, and bag inside and dropped them near the door.

"My mystery man," Nicole said, looking around the living room of the suite. "Everything is so beautiful!"

"You're beautiful, Nicole." Jared pulled her to him in a long embrace. His familiar clean, masculine scent excited her. He tilted her chin down and kissed her lightly on the forehead. He brushed her cheeks softly, slowly, with the backs of his hands and let his fingers slide down her arched throat to the round fullness of her breasts. Continuing down Nicole's body, Jared cupped her perfect butt in his hands and gently kissed her top lip, then her bottom lip, before parting them and entering her mouth with his tongue. They deeply explored each other's mouths until Nicole thought she would reach total satisfaction from the kiss alone.

Jared led Nicole into the candlelit bedroom. He shut the door and positioned Nicole so she faced the full-length mirror affixed to the back of the door.

"Look at yourself, baby. I must be the luckiest man in the world." Jared stood directly behind Nicole, the hair on his broad chest tickling the smooth curve of her back. His arms encircled her waist as he ran his tongue along the nape of her neck. She watched as he moved his hands slowly up her body and unclasped the front of her bra, letting her breasts fall free. He ran his fingers up and over her nipples, then back down to her hips. Nicole watched his every move. She felt like an actress starring in an erotic movie. The effect was titillating. Jared saw the pleasure in her eyes reflected back at him.

"Are you watching, baby?" he asked as he slid one hand down inside her panties and caressed her left nipple with the other. She watched as he parted the soft, downy hair between her legs and found her deep, pink, throbbing core.

Nicole moaned as Jared massaged her ever so slowly until she was slippery wet, and her moaning grew more intense. Nicole's breath was coming now in quick, short pants. Jared's fingers rubbed gently, but faster and faster as he sensed Nicole approaching ecstasy.

Nicole closed her eyes and reached behind her to hold on to Jared's hips for support.

"Open your eyes, baby," he whispered. He slid her panties down over her ankles, then knelt down in front of Nicole, between her and the mirror. "I want you to see me do it to you." He placed his hands on her ass and pulled her to his full, wet lips. Jared ran his tongue slowly over her mound of swollen hardness, lingering at the tip until Nicole grabbed his shoulders, arched backward, and screamed his name. He thrust his tongue inside her until he felt her shudder from the release.

Jared rose and scooped Nicole up and carried her to the bed. He stood over her trembling body and announced that he was now ready to reveal the secret. He then let the pale blue towel fall, exposing his enormous erection, then said, "I'm all yours, baby."

### ❦ bell hooks ❦

# Bone Black

*On September 25, 1952, the world was first introduced to bell hooks, née Gloria Watkins. After getting her Ph.D. from the University of California, Santa Cruz, she came to City College in New York to teach Cultural Criticism and Analysis. This passage is from the first of her two autobiographical works,* Bone Black: Memories of Girlhood; *her other major collection of autobiographical writings is called* Wounds of Passion: A Writing Life.

MASTURBATION IS SOMETHING SHE HAS NEVER HEARD ANYONE talk about girls doing. Like so many spaces of fun and privilege in their world, it is reserved for the boy child—the one whose growing passion for sexuality can be celebrated, talked about with smiles of triumph and pleasure. A boy coming into awareness of his sexuality is on his way to manhood—it is an important moment. The stained sheets that show signs of his having touched his body are flags of victory. They—the girls—have no such moments. Sexuality is something that will be done to them, something they have to fear. It can bring unwanted pregnancy. It can turn one into a whore. It is a curse. It will ruin a young girl's life, pull her into pain again and again, into childbirth, into welfare, into all sorts of longings that will never be satisfied. Again and again they tell their mother she does not need to worry about them. They are not sexual. They will not get pregnant, will not bring home babies for her to take care of. They do not actually say We are not sexual for the very use of the word *sexual* might suggest knowledge — they make sexuality synonymous with pregnancy, with being a whore, a slut.

When she finds pleasure touching her body, she knows that they will think it wrong; that it is something to keep hidden, to do in secret. She is ashamed, ashamed that she comes home from school wanting to lie in bed touching the wet dark hidden parts of her body, ashamed that she lies awake nights touching herself, moving her hands, her fingers deeper and deeper inside, inside the place of woman's pain and misery, the place men want to enter, the place babies come through — ashamed of the pleasure.

When she finally has a room all to herself she can go there when no one notices and enjoy her body. This pleasure is her secret and her shame. She denies to herself that she is being sexual. She refuses to think about it. Males are not the object of her lust. She does not touch herself thinking about their penises moving inside her, the wetness of their ejaculations. It is her own wetness that the fingers seek. It is the moment she thinks of, not as orgasm, for she does nor know the word, but as the moment of climbing a tall place and reaching the top. This is what she longs for. There she finds a certain contentedness and bliss. It is this bliss the fingers guide her to. Like the caves she dreamed about in childhood it is a place of refuge, a sanctuary.

Like all secret pleasure she finds the hiding hard. She knows her sisters have begun to wonder about the moments alone in the dark cool room, the times in bed reading when they are outside. They watch her, waiting. They open the door fast. They pull the covers quickly before she can free her hands. They bear witness to her pleasure and her shame. Her pleasure in the body, her shame at being found out. They threaten to tell, they can't wait to tell. She prepares her denial. She goes over and over it in her head. Like a party ending because the lights are suddenly turned on she knows the secret moments are gone, the dark, the pleasure, the deep cool ecstasy.

### ❧ CHARLES JOHNSON ❧

# Middle Passage

*In addition to his critically acclaimed novels and short stories,
Charles Johnson has published essays, book reviews, and two
collections of drawings and has written for various educational
television series. He is a richly imaginative, daringly complex
writer whose work consistently manages the difficult feat of being
at once thrilling and tender, fatalistic and funny. This is from Middle Passage, which won the 1990 National Book Award. Charles
Johnson is the Pollack Professor of English at the University of
Washington in Seattle. I chose this excerpt as an excellent example of using erotica to end a novel.*

I STOOD WHERE I WAS, RELIEVED AND SMILING, BUT I WONDERED
what to do next, where to begin, how to close the physical distance of the last few months. Furthermore, how could I tell her
that Santos might stay overnight if he came to visit? How could
we keep him away? More importantly, how in heaven's name
would we *feed* him?

"Are those flowers for me?" she asked. Again, she flashed that
foolish, fetching, teasingly erotic smile. "Bring them here."

I sat down beside her, kissed the cheek she turned up toward me, then sat twiddling my thumbs. Meanwhile, Isadora took a whiff of the flowers strong enough to suck a few petals into her nose. She let the bouquet fall to the floor and turned to me after moistening her lips with the tip of her tongue. Placing her left hand on my shoulder to hold me still, she used her right to grip the top of my slops, and pulled. Buttons popped off my breeches like buckshot, pinging against the bulkhead.

"Isadora," I asked in a pinched voice, "are you sure you want to do this? We can sit and read Scripture or poetry together, if you wish."

She made answer by rising to her bare feet, shoving me back onto the bed, and tugging off my boots and breeches. By heaven, I thought, still water runs *deep*. Who'd have dreamed these depths of passion were in a prim Boston schoolteacher? She was so sexually bold I began to squirm. I mean, *I* was the sailor, wasn't I? Abruptly, my own ache for detumescence, for a little Late Night All Right, took hold of me, beginning at about my fourth rib and flying downward. Soon we both had our hands inside each other's clothes. How long it had been since someone held me, touched me with something other than a boot heel or the back of their hand! And she, so much slimmer—pulling the gown over her head—was to me a figure of such faint-inducing grace and Odysseus would have swallowed the ocean whole, if need be, to swim to her side. I kissed the swale by her collarbone and trailed my lips along her neck. Then, afraid of what I might do next, I slid my fingers under my thighs and sat on my hands.

Isadora twirled slowly on her toes, letting me see all of her. Now that she had my undivided attention, she asked, "Well, what do you think?"

"I'm not thinking."

"Good."

"But the animals. Can't you send them outside?"

"Rutherford!"

"At least cover up the birdcage."

"Don't worry, he's blind." Her voice was husky. "Just lie still."

Knowing nothing else to do, I obeyed. Isadora climbed over my outstretched legs, lowered herself to my waist, and began pushing her hips back and forth, whispering, "No, don't move." I wondered: Where did she learn this? Against her wishes, I did move, easing her onto her side, then placed my hand where it wanted to go. We groped awkwardly for a while, but something was wrong. Things were not progressing as smoothly as they were supposed to. ("Your elbow's in my eyeball," said I; "Sorry," said she; "Hold on, I think I've got a charley horse.") I was out of practice. Rusty. My body's range of motion was restricted by the bruises I had taken at sea, yet my will refused to let go. I peeled off my blouse, determined to lay the ax to the root like a workman spitting on his palms before settling down to the business at hand; but, hang it, my memories of the Middle Passage kept coming back, reducing the velocity of my desire, its violence, and in place of my longing for feverish love-making left only a vast stillness that felt remarkably full, a feeling that, just now, I wanted our futures blended, not our limbs, our histories perfectly twined for all time, not our flesh. Desire was too much of a wound, a rip of insufficiency and incompleteness that kept us, despite our proximity, constantly apart, like metals with an identical charge.

I stopped, and stared quite helplessly at Isadora, who said, "I thought this was what you wanted?"

"Isadora, I . . . don't think so."

She studied my face, saying nothing, and in this wordless exchange felt the difference in me. It coincided, I sensed by slow degrees, with one in herself, for in her disheveled blankets we realized this Georgia fatwood furnace we were stoking was not the release either of us needed. Rather, what she and I wanted most after so many adventures was the incandescence, very chaste, of an embrace that would outlast the Atlantic's bone-chilling cold. Accordingly, she lowered her head to my shoulder, as a sister might. Her warm fingers, busy as moths a moment before, were quiet on my chest. Mine, on her hair as the events of the last half year overtook us. Isadora drifted toward rest, nestled snugly beside me, where she would remain all night while we, forgetful of ourselves, gently crossed the Flood, and countless seas of suffering.

# Mosquito

*Gayl Jones was born in Kentucky in 1949. She attended Con-*
*necticut College and Brown University. All of her books have re-*
*ceived critical acclaim. They include* Corregidora, Eva's Man, The
Healing, *and* Liberating Voices: Oral Tradition in African American
Literature. *This excerpt is taken from my favorite of her novels,*
Mosquito, *the story and adventures of Sojourner Nadine Jane*
*Johnson (aka Mosquito), a truck driver in a south Texas border*
*town.*

### Monkey Bread's Story

Do you take John Hollywood to be your lawful husband?

We was playing and so I said I took John Hollywood to be my
lawful husband and promised to love and cherish him. We rented
us a house because he was pretending to have himself a good fac-
tory job making business machines and I was pretending to have
me a good job in one of them department stores downtown, and
them was the years when they didn't hire African-American peo-
ples to work as clerks in them stores, at least not in that part of the
country. Them that owned they own little stores could work as

clerks in them. He used his real name, John Hollywood, but me I renamed myself Casablanca, like the title of that movie, and I kept thinking it was a grand name, a grander name than Monkey Bread. John Hollywood wanted to call me by my true name, but I didn't think that my true name was a good enough name to be John Hollywood's wife. So I became Casablanca Hollywood.

We pretended like John Hollywood was a good Christian because in that little community good men was supposed to be good Christians, and pretended that he was the best man in the world, and who could marry better? Who couldn't be in love with such a man? I don't know whether he pretended that I was the best woman in the world. Even with my name Casablanca.

Then, after we was married, we pretended that we had us a short weekend honeymoon to Mammoth Cave, Kentucky, where a lot of newlyweds had honeymooned and come back telling glory stories.

We pretended a little neighborhood cave was Mammoth Cave, and when we wasn't pretending we was husbands and wives, we was pretending that we was guides in that cave, and we talked about how we'd add more passages in that cave and would discover more passages in that cave, passages that hadn't been explored by any of them other newlyweds. We had us a good time in that little cave and just like newlyweds come back telling everybody how wonderful us honeymoon, though we was telling imaginary people, and we was telling them about how the Indians—cause we called them Indians then—made that cave, and how they had that cave before the white men come and commercialized it, 'cept we didn't use that word *commercialized:*

Then, 'cause I'd never met John Hollywood's folks, we traveled to his house to meet his folks, and pretended that they lived in North Dakota rather than on the other street and pretended that they hadn't been able to come to the wedding 'cause they lived in North Dakota and there we was in Kentucky, you know. So we saved up money, or pretending we was saving up money, so's we could go to North Dakota.

I don't know how long we pretended. I called him the good husband, and he'd sit on the porch with me at night and watch the moon light up my face. We pretended it was the moon. I liked to comb his hair with my fingers and kiss the top of his head, and I liked to tell our imaginary people how wonderful a husband, and we'd pretend we was drinking beer though it weren't nothing but root beer, Nadine. (I decided I'd put you in my story, although I don't think you even knew John Hollywood in them days.) We'd drink beer which was root beer and talk about Mammoth Cave. I don't know if they Jim Crowed Mammoth Cave in them days, but that's where we pretended we'd honeymooned. We also pretended that we went up to Cincinnati to the zoo and to Louisville to the state fair. We even talked about Lying us some children although they's imaginary children. I know what you's thinking. Nadine. Naw, we didn't do that in that cave.

Then we pretended that we traveled by bus to North Dakota, though we took us a bus ride all around the city. John Hollywood held my hand and I slept on his shoulder. We'd saved us a lot of money so's we could take that trip to North Dakota. We rode on the back of the bus, 'cause they Jim Crowed them buses in them days.

I asked John Hollywood. What your father do?

In the winter he work on the railroad, in the summer he a lumberman.

We held hands, and then we got off the bus and walked out into the country, though it was still the city, but we was pretending it was the country, you know, Nadine. and I pretended that I seen my first deer, you know, like they might have in the country of North Dakota. Then we walked on one of them little dirt roads, the dust sticking to our shoes. We walked across stones and seen a crab on its back in the sun. Then we come into the clearing, and they was three little girls with bowl haircuts playing on the porch. John Hollywood's sisters Lira, Lolly, and Lola, I couldn't tell them apart. John Hollywood introduced me to his parents as his new bride. They knew we was just play-acting so they shook hands with me and hugged me and called me pretty, 'cause you always calls new brides pretty.

We rested and ate there. We had us corn and venison stew and apple pie. Naw, Nadine, it wasn't no real venison stew, we was just play-acting that it was venison stew. I fell in love with John Hollywood's family and his little sisters and we all played us a game of catch in the yard. Then his daddy went to work and the little girls went off to school and John Hollywood went into town and I stayed with his mama who I thought was a quiet, beautiful woman, and she kinda reminded me of one of them Indian womens 'cause she had that long hair that she wore in just like them Indian women, and she kept play-acting with us 'cause she said she wished that she could have traveled down from North Dakota to come to our wedding, and then she told me that John Hollywood gave her a picture of me and that she was pleased with his choice in a woman. I didn't know that grownups could pretend so good as that.

Is he taking care of you? she asked.

Yes, ma'am.

And you take care of him? Yes. I see you do.

Then we washed the dishes together and went out to the garden for tomatoes and set them on the windowsill, and she had all kinds of plants in her garden and knew the names of them just like you say about Deigadina. And we took a walk together and she told me that they had only one movie house in that little town, and figured that my name being Casablanca that I must like movies. Do you swim? There's a wonderful creek.

Course there wasn't no creek at all around there. When I told her I didn't swim—which was a lie—she told me that maybe John would teach me. Then she asked me how long we'd be able to stay, just like I was a real newlywed, and wished I could stay and visit them longer, and then we come back and sit on the porch, and John Hollywood returned from town. And his mama went back in the house to do her housecleaning.

How was town? I asked.

Ain't a lot changed, he said. Then we pretended we was at the movies and he sat with his arm around my shoulders' like we'd see the teenage boys do, then his mama bought us some hamburgers and some of them little apple pies and some Coca-Cola. We had us a picnic and pretended it was us first picnic, which it was.

Even as a little boy John Hollywood were real muscular and kinda remind me of a man. Didn't remind me of Dick in Dick and Jane, but reminded me more of Dick in "Dick Tracy." Except even more a manly man, but he weren't nothing but a little boy.

I don't know what else us pretended. I asked him if he'd ever thought of settling in North Dokota, but he said it weren't nothing there but the railroad and lumber.

Your mama look like a Indian, I says.

She is a Indian he says. And then he told me 'bout his grandfather, a medicine man, and give me a belt of deerskin supposed to be made by his grandfather. I still got that belt, Nadine, and sometimes I thinks it's got real medicine in it.

I ain't know if that a true story he mama a Indian, but you know, Nadine, that's when I started to look at John Hollywood a little different, like they was something a little mysterious about him, even though he were the same John Hollywood. And he the same John Hollywood.

# The Cotillion, or, One Good Bull Is Half the Herd

*John Oliver Killens (1916–1987) was a novelist, playwright, and songwriter. He went to law school, fought in World War II, lectured widely, taught creative writing, and was a cofounder of the Harlem Writers Guild. I have included a brief excerpt from his 1970 novel,* The Cotillion, or, One Good Bull Is Half the Herd *(nominated for a Pulitzer Prize) because I think he is too little remembered today.*

HE KISSED HER EYES, EACH IN THEIR OWN DARK TURN. "My Yoruba! Black and beautiful Yoruba! How many times did I walk the roads of Yoruba—land in faraway Abeokuta—Ibadan—" He kissed her mouth again. "And thought of you, sweet Yoruba—looked for you in the soft eyes of Yoruba women—" He kissed her cheeks. "All dressed they were in blue they were—Soft blue dresses." He kissed the corners of her mouth. "The way they walked—greatgoda'mighty! The way they walked!" He kissed her ears. And he turned her on with talk and kisses. "But it was always you—you—Yoruba—you—you! I thought of, always looked for, you—Sometimes, I remembered you as you used to be at six, seven, eight years old—And yet I looked for you, the woman you, in Benin City, as if a miracle could happen."

When she was with her Captain, she needed no strong drinks, or pot, to turn her on; he could take her on a trip with words, set her sailing out to sea, with verbs and nouns and adjectives. He kissed her on her lips again, and she felt rivulets of sweetest feelings run the course of her entire being. And she held on to him, in a kind of desperation now, the sea was really choppy, and she'd never learned to swim. Now she felt the Captain's gentle hands all over her, talking all the while, "You, Yoruba, you, Yoruba," all the private secret places of her, tenderly did he explore. She thought she heard herself screaming, but not a sound came forth. Save me, Captain! Save me! Save me from sinking down.

She felt herself being lifted gently firmly from the sea into the Captain's arms. He laid her on the Captain's bunk, the couch. She felt herself as in a dream being dispossessed of her under-things, she thought she hoped she mouthed a feeble protest. When he laid her back upon the couch, she thought that she would truly sink this time as the great awful terrible wonderful waves washed over her, gaining force each time, and she reached up to him. Save me! Save me! Take me! Take me! And he took her, and they rode the waves together, moving ever toward the shore, they took the mighty waves together. Higher! Higher! Higher! Painful, painful, was this first ride for her, blood and pain and joyous feelings, all converging as they rode the swells like great surf-riders. But being one who naturally knew the ocean, he was the Captain and seaworthy, and, of course, he reached the shore ahead of her, as she thrashed amongst the waves, heaving, sighing, breathing heavy, in all her inexperience, in an awful desperation, thought the world was lost forever; so he stayed the tides for moments, long and agonizing moments, and came back to bring her with him. She, floundering and faltering, thinking: I can't make it! I'll never make it! I'll die here among the waves, amidst the blood and sweat and tears! Weeping now in great frustration. But the Captain firm and gentle, tough and tender all the way. He, the wise and patient Captain, whispering: "Take it easy, I'm here with you. Wouldn't leave you for the world." They began again together. He, her one and only Captain, kissed her eyes, salty-sweet with tears, kissed her trembly vacillating lips. No! No! Yes! Yes! Let us try another time another day. Never ever again! His dear sophisticated tongue caressed her ears, "Shh—be quiet—" tongued deliciously her breasts, her darling bellybutton, her tippy-toes atingle now, his sensitive fingers, touching everything now, like a great maestro conjuring exquisite music from a masterpiece of instrument, all the secret private only-for-him places, touching all and tuning up and turning on. A symphony of feelings, an ebony rhapsody, "Oh yes! Yes! Yes! Lumumba!" Softly whispering to her, "Take it easy! Take it easy! Take it easy! My Yoruba!" She the girl, Yoruba, thinking, Can I? Can I? Will I ever? I can't! I can't! I can't! We can—we can—As they stroked for shore again. Slower, slower was the painful rhythm. Oh yes we can—Oh yes we can—We must—We must—You see—my lovely queen—we did—Yes, but—yes, but—I understand, my darling Ruba, it will never be like this again—You'll see—next time we'll really make the shore together—together—together—always together. Without pain we'll make the shore.

Now they lay there panting in the sweet smell of the salty sea, the salty bloody smell the virgin soil of love had made. Lay there where the blessed beachhead was established, as the ebbing tide receded. Lay there basking 'neath a rainbow at the end of love's horizon which was also the beginning.

Now the Captain's eyes surveyed the lovely landscape, as the dear princess slept serenely on the Captain's bunk—breathing softly, fearing nothing with the Captain's arms embracing her. He had pulled back all the covers without the dear queen's knowledge. She only half heard him now as his voice began to bring her back from her exquisite slumber. She, the girl, Yoruba, was in that never-ever land between sleep and wake like the moments in between moon-down and sunrise, when the dogs begin to move around and the chicks begin to stir out in the sticks, just before the city lights go off. The newsboy and the milkman's time.

She heard Lumumba as if from far away, coming closer, fading further, now closer, now further. "Your breasts are like what? Plump cupcakes with darksweet rare grapes at the center. Or are they cone-shaped honeycombs tipped with wild sweet muscadines. Your hips so darkly round and black and brown, a million shades and sweetly slim. The sweet slope of your stomach around your sunken bellybutton. Your hair so dark and shortly cropped and pubic and shining blue-black triangle of our love — the pubic hair is the loveliest dearest most exquisite hair in all the world, there is no hair like this, there never was." He laughed. "They should cover up the tophead hair of womankind and let the lovely hair of maidenhead be brought to light."

When she awakened fully, the modest child let out a squeal of very deep embarrassment. She quickly reached for the Captain's bedsheet and covered her embarrassment. The Captain laughed and laughed and laughed. Until she slapped the Captain's face.

They say we always hurt the ones we love.

◁] JAMAICA KINCAID [▷

# The Autobiography
# of My Mother

*Jamaica Kincaid was born in St. John's, Antigua, in 1949 and emigrated to the United States in 1966. Her works of fiction include* At the Bottom of the River, Annie John, Lucy, *and* The Autobiography of My Mother. *She lives with her family in Vermont.*

THE INEVITABLE IS NO LESS A SHOCK JUST BECAUSE IT IS inevitable. I was sitting, late one day, in a small shaded area behind the house, where some flowers were planted, though this place could not be called a garden, for not much care was applied to it. The sun had not yet set completely; it was just at that moment when the creatures of the day are quiet but the creatures of the night have not quite found their voice. It was that time of day when all you have lost is heaviest in your mind: your mother, if you have lost her; your home, if you have lost it; the voices of people who might have loved you or who you only wish had loved you; the places in which something good, something you cannot forget, happened to you. Such feelings of longing and loss are heaviest just in that light. Day is almost over, night has almost begun. I did not wear undergarments anymore, I found them uncomfortable, and as I sat there I touched various parts of my body, sometimes absentmindedly, sometimes with a purpose in mind. I was running the fingers of my left hand through the small thick patch of hair between my legs and thinking of my life as I had lived it so far, fifteen years of it now, and I saw that Monsieur LaBatte was standing not far off from me, looking at me. He did not move away in embarrassment and I, too, did not run away in embarrassment. We held each other's gaze. I removed my fingers from between my legs and brought them up to my face, I wanted to smell myself. It was the end of the day, my odor was quite powerful. This scene of me placing my hand between my legs and then enjoying the smell of myself and Monsieur LaBatte watching me lasted until the usual sudden falling of the dark, and so when he came closer to me and asked me to remove my clothes, I said, quite sure of myself, knowing what it was I wanted, that it was too dark, I could not see. He took me to the room in which he counted his money, the money that was only some of the money he had. It was a dark room and so he kept a small lamp always lighted in it. I took off my clothes and he took off his clothes. He was the first man I had ever seen unclothed and he surprised me: the body of a man is not what makes him desirable, it is what his body might make you feel when it touches you that is the thrill, anticipating what his body will make you feel, and then the reality becomes better than the anticipation and the world has a wholeness to it, a wholeness with a current running through it, a current of pure pleasure. But when I first saw him, his hands hanging at his side, not yet caressing my hair, not yet inside me, not yet bringing the small risings that were my breasts toward his mouth, not yet opening my mouth wider to place his tongue even deeper in my mouth, the limp folds of the flesh on his stomach, the hardening flesh between his legs, I was surprised at how unbeautiful he was all by himself, just standing there; it was anticipation that was the thrill, it was anticipation that kept me enthralled. And the force of him inside me, inevitable as it was, again came as a shock, a long sharp line of pain that then washed over me with the broadness of a wave, a long sharp line of pleasure: and to each piercing that he made inside me, I made a cry that was the same cry, a cry of sadness, for without making of it something it really was not I was not the same person I had been before. He was not a man of love, I did not need him to be. When he was through with me and I with him, he lay on top of me, breathing indifferently; his mind was on other things. On a small shelf at his back I could see he had lined up many coins, their sides turned heads up; they bore the face of a king.

In the room where I slept, the room with the floor of dirt, I poured water into a small tin basin and washed the thin crust of blood that had dried between my legs and down the inside of my legs. This blood was not a mystery to me, I knew why it was there, I knew what had just happened to me. I wanted to see what I looked like, but I could not. I felt myself; my skin felt smooth, as if it had just been oiled and freshly polished. The place between my legs ached, my breasts ached, my lips ached, my wrists ached; when he had not wanted me to touch him, he had placed his own large hands over my wrists and kept them pinned to the floor; when my cries had distracted him, he had clamped my lips shut with his mouth. It was through all the parts of my body that ached that I relived the deep pleasure I had just experienced. When I awoke the next morning I did not feel I had slept at all; I felt as if I had only lost consciousness and I picked up where I had left off in my ache of pleasure.

## ❧ CLARENCE MAJOR ❧

# All-Night Visitors

*Clarence Major teaches at the University of California, Davis, but he only ended up there after spending a time working at a number of schools across the country. The New York Times continues to notice his work, but no one else seems to. I picked this passage from his great novel All-Night Visitors, but if you really like it, you should take a look at his poetry.*

ANITA IS WHIPPING HER TIGHT PUSSY ON ME LIKE MAD! WE ARE IN her dark beautiful apartment, with a little wine that has warmed her, I think, more than it has me. "I want the light on," I say, and get up; the shock of my sudden movement, leaving her, stuns her. I come back. The bright three-way lamp, a new dimension on her caramel-colored, firm, lean body. The taut little tits with their large rich dark *dark* red berries, some sweet nipples. The gentle yellow lights drive mathematical light sets, like beautiful *tupu* sounds of Coltrane. My spongy, sore, moist sword, as I come back to the bed, dripping her juice along the way, the sweet goodness of it all soothing my limbs; I happily pat my stomach, singing a couple of bars from something new by James

Brown as I jump on the bed, over her now, growling like a dog, "GGRRRRRRRRRR," and imagining, even how it looks graphically in cartoons, or here, which is also a kind of cartoon of love, my soft black dick, by now completely stunted into a virginal softness, hanging there, and Anita goes, "Lazy nigger, you!" And her wide mouth, those big eyes, sparkling, her white *white* teeth glowing, spotless, virtuous teeth. "I'm dog—GRRRRRRRRRR bowwow! BOW-WOW! BOW-WOW WOW WOW WOW WOW!" I am in her face, and her head is turned sideways; she's looking with those big Lil Armstrong–jazzdays eyes at me, as if to say, "Who're you supposed to be *now*? What kinda new game is this, little boy? *My my*, men are always boys! Boastful, silly, self-centered little boys, who want somebody to jack them off all the time!"

She giggles, the unclear voice of Donovan carries its weight equal in space, timing our senses, from the FM radio. Her big red tongue shoots out, touches my nose. It is good that I am able to enjoy these moments with Anita, despite all the past contamination between us! She runs her long (she has an *extra* long, extra red, extra *active*) tongue around my cheeks, quickly licks my lips, but I am still a pompous dog ready to bark again, when her hard, long, firm hand intrudes in the soft, baggy, damp, hairy area of my semen-smelling fruit picker. The conduct of her dry hand always astonishes me, as it delights. She is still giggling. I am delighted, of course, whenever she touches my dick, I like it in a very civil way, not just a natural magnet, magic way. She puts me in large swimming pools of myself weighty with *supreme delight*, despite the slight roughness of her hand. Anita's hand is not rough because she's been washing dishes, sweeping floors, or ironing clothes—they're rough in a *natural* way. She is a creamy thing, *hard* all over. Her little tits are stiff cups that stand firmly, like prudent sentries, looking with dark steadiness in opposite directions. Her stomach is firmer than any stomach, male or female, that I've ever seen. There isn't one inch of fat on her anywhere unless we consider her earlobes fat. Donovan is doing "Mellow Yellow"; as I gently let myself down beside her, she's saying, "Lazzzy lazy nigger, *humhumhum,*" still holding my soft copper-headed dick with a kind of playful sense of disgust. For a moment I feel slightly ashamed that my bonanza detector remains, even in her active hand, serene. She is simply shaking it back and forth, and now asking, *"What's this?"* She smells clean, fleshy clean, she always does. So gently soapy-smelling, not strong with some overdose of peakily cheap perfume!

She is already on her elbow, looking down at me by now, smacking her lips, going, "Tut tut tut— What am I gonna do with you, nigger, huh? You're a mess—*won't* it get hard?" *"Be nice* to it, Anita, baby, it'll do anything you want it to do . . ." Yes, it has been a long time since she's given me that sacred rite she is such a master at performing. I'm thinking, Why should I torture poor Mr. ex-Perpendicular any longer, tonight, in her dry hole? She gets up to her knees, and I deliberately say nothing because I know from past experience that Anita does not like for me to ask her to suck it, though when she volunteers, she has proven to be unbeatable at getting to the essence of the act.

I remember now as she is about to suck it, she knows that at least turning it around in her mouth, swiveling it, whirling it, rotating it with her thick, long tongue, makes it hard as bookends; and vigorous, so powerful, in fact, that I've rocked and almost unhinged her torso from such long pithy severe sessions of pure slippery fucking, pushing one juicy hour to the rhythm of music, into another, right here in this bed. And I suspect now she thinks she'll get me hard and *then* stretch out on her back, her brittle pussy hairs twisting together there, damply, at the mouth of the jewel, hiding that ruthless, hungry, merciless gem! that gobbles and gobbles, eats at me—rather, lies more or less in repose as *I*, out of deep meanings of the self, feel compelled to work myself to death, so to speak, to fill up its crater! But that ain't what's happening this time—she doesn't know it yet, but she's going to swivel it, rotate it, nibble it, lick it, gently chew on it, playfully bite it, turn and turn it in the spitkingdom of herself, dance it with her tongue, spank it with juice, excite it to huge precipices without bursting it out of its tense axis of delight; she's going to hold it in honor with both brown hands, as it dips, tosses, as it ascends, in all oh all ranges of mind states! Yes, it is my mind! Equal, that is, to every level of myself . . .

I know I can turn her *off* if I say One Word now. That's the last thing in the world I want to do now as I feel the weight of her knees adjusting between mine. "Put this pillow under you—" She's being clinical; OK, if she wants to be that way, it'll still be good. I feel how I deliberately relax every muscle I can consciously focus on with my mind. She wiggles her firm ass, adjusting it somewhere on her heels, her arms inside the warm soft area of my thighs, I feel the hairs of them. She takes a deep breath; I can smell the air of the ruby we drank drift up to my nostrils. Sound: the slow wet movement of her strong red tongue moving over her lips, mopping away the dryness. Like most of her body's exterior, her lips are usually very dry. Only two spots, exceptions, I can think of: the areas around the edges of her scalp, the crevices between her thighs and where the mound of her pussy begins to rise, are usually warm and moist. As I lift my narrow ass, holding myself in a loop, she slides the big pillow beneath me, I sink down into the conquering softness, her busy automatic-acting fingers tickle the rooty area at the base of this selfish generative Magic Flute of mine, pull and squeeze my sagging sensitive balls. She coughs, clears her throat. I hear the smack of her tongue between her lips again. I have my eyes closed, soon I'll feel the slow, warm, nerve-wracking sweet fuck of the pensive mouth beginning . . .

This hesitation. I know it is coming. Her mouth has not yet touched the ruby head of my *dick*. The moment of waiting, the anxiety of it builds like musical improvisations in my bones, my membranes, the heat, blood energy in me; I continue to try to keep it all very still, cool, I am not even trying to concentrate on hardening up my ecstasy-weapon, this dear *uume* to the emissive glory of life itself! And for once Anita doesn't seem impatient, she isn't pumping it, bungling, and jacking it, trying to make it instantly hard—I suspect she's going to make it really great this time. She can be absolutely wonderful, when she wants to! The anticipation of these moments, of a kind of antagonism of sweet memory of the best times, is overpowering. It takes all the will in my being to lie here, still, the corporeality of myself, in the spit-slick heady memory of it . . .

(It is only at these moments, of course, that this particular "movement" of the symphony of life is so beautifully important, all-consuming . . . Equal to the working moments when I am excited by the energetic, rich growth of a concept I am able to articulate! Or my sudden ability to construct bookshelves, or create a silly wacky lovely painting, equal to anything that I do involving the full disclosure of myself! I hesitate to say equal to my ability to handle those firearms in Vietnam, against those nameless human collages that fell in the distance, like things, but maybe even equal to that, too . . .)

The hot nude hole of her mouth, *oh God it is so goooooood!!!* slides now, caressingly, dry at first, but she's excreting saliva like cunt juice, her firm hands stretching out, in slow motion, sliding up my flat stomach, my gentle spongy dick blowing up, expand-ing at a pace equal to the tension in her lips behind the root of her tongue, getting hot as the crevices of her gums, the deliber-ately slow sinking of her mouth still coming down to the very base of my seed-giver, gently, but firmly engulfing it, in all of its lazy softness the nerve-ends of my whole ass, my nuts, my thighs are fructifying! The meaty warmth of her velvety lined interior begins to climb just as slowly; Mr. Prick is anxious to quickly reach the full and painful proportion of its promise, but I fight that drive by applying more and more deliberation to my restraint, under the magic, almost weightless touch of her fingers as she adroitly glides them down, tripping through the hairs of my stomach. She need not hold my *uume* with her hands any longer. "He" is trying too hard to make headway in his headiness! He holds himself up; I refuse to let the progressive bastard gristle up to the prolific point where he is like some giant tendon, though Anita might (if she weren't unusually patient right now) *like* that; O motion, joy, oh *shit*, this is TOO MUCH! The still missiling motion of the circle of her tight mouth, restrainingly prolonged, up—up! I can feel the inelastic cords of my inner tissues pulling in a complex of nerves, pulling, as her strong Big Black Woman, Mighty Nile, African energetic tough lips, the muscles in them quivering, the lengthy moist spongy-porous tongue gently milking the base of my valve, Mr. Hammer's underbelly, milks fruitfully, in a slow rhythm. My eyes are still closed, I am trying not to settle my mind anywhere, it tries for a moment to drift to the greasy magazine of a gun I was examining one day, sitting propped against another guy's back, at the edge of a rice paddy, and I don't know why. I want to *stay* right here, with her, focused on every protrusion, every cord, abstract circle of myself, of her every "feeling," every hurling, every fleshy spit-rich convexity, mentally centered in all the invisible "constructs" of myself, right here, where she and I now form, perform an orchestra she is conducting in juicy floodtides; stay *in* her woman's construction, her work, her togetherness, the rich procreating like magic of her every touch as—more and more against my will—my *kok* protracts, *swells*, lengthens, perpetuatingly jumpy with fertility, as her permeable mouth decreases its gentle grip in exact ratio to Dick's eminent *strong* polarity. I love her for her reflective, melancholy approach to this fine art! So seldom does she take this much care to do it properly.

My serpent is just fatty-hard, but extra long, redundantly so! It is *best* this way, if I can manage to keep it from stiffening to the point where the nerves are minimized somehow. I feel the mouth-motions of her workings, the salivary warmth of her slow, pensive chewing at the *acutely sensitive head*, where the loose skin has slid back, the rich, thick nerve-ends in the thin layers of this loose skin, she lets spit run down slowly around this Bridegroom in his moment of heaven, the warm secreted water from the prolific glands of her taste bud–sensitive mouth, I feel these oh so slow careful and skillful movements, the deliberate soft scraping and raking of her beautiful strong teeth across the tender texture of the rim of the head, gently bathing with spit the prepuce's densely nervepacked walls, which rub these ends of my luckily uninhibited penis. She is concentrating on the head of it, and she can do this for so long it drives me *mad* with porous, beautiful pleasure. She will nibble here, suck one or two times, stop, let it rest limp, aching, in the soft warm cave of her rich dark purple "construct," saliva mixing easily with the slow sebaceous secretion, my own male liquid lubricant, *smegma*, washing around in her grip—a gentle but well-controlled clasp! Then, she might take a gentle but playful plunge *down*, straight down, down, sinking down faster than she's so far moved, the dick head exploding up into all that wet, warm slime, it's running down, profusely, the tunnel-sinking sense of it, the sounds of the cool capful of wind speeding away giving way to this cravefeeding, just the hallelujah-warm, narcotic feeling of the drop, as my dick thickens, pushes out—the lengthy pole emitting into her muscles, and tonsils, the juicy soup of my penis glands, the sheath, now in this plunging motion stretched in this hymn of heat to frantic, mad ends! Two more strokes like this and she can finish me. I would shoot a hurricane of seeds into her, falling out convulsively, palmus, in nervous-twitching; *but* Anita isn't trying to finish me off this time, get it over. She's going to be good to me, but I *cannot* keep myself from the submissive fear that she might suddenly bring it to an end, and it can be very painful if it is done incorrectly. Instinctively, Anita knows this. This knowledge is in the very pores of her skin: she is the knowledgeable Mother of a deep wisdom, intrinsic in her every chromosome.

Yes.

*God!!!* Yes! She can sustain me, even as I lay pitched on this *brink*, she controls it all. The way I'm beginning to whimper, groan, beyond my own control, she controls it all. With her mouth, she is screwing the head of my dick, around and around. She is worrying it now, from side to side, clasping it, increasing and decreasing the pressure, the circles of my mind follow some rhythm she is leading in this voracity. My ass is beginning to throb under the acute, tremendous, mesmeric workings of her facsimile-pussy which has the irresistible kind of skill the lower mouth of ecstatic agony, also a spicy feast, with good lips, does not have, because it lacks this *mobility*. I lie still, the rich body-pungency, the

105

fuck-fragrance of ourselves in my senses, the dry taste of my tongue; as I lie here, my palms face up, the smell of rich black sweet cunt filling the room, the door of her mouth, the wet-smell of my own pungent body fluids that escape her jaws, dripping down into the hairs around this cylindrical, pendulous totem pole, Anita's rhythm upon it begins to increase . . .

I worry. Please, baby! Take it easy; but I am not speaking. A few muscles of fear harden in my stomach but I manipulate them back to peace. *Be quiet body*, but she now masculinely grips it, the excited columns of its interior pressed together, the cavernous tissues throbbing, like my head is throbbing, the roots of my hair, my toes are twitching, like this wonderful up-standing organ, she is holding in its wet harmony, as she treats the head like it's a pop-sicle. Anita has her hand just below the bulbo-cavenous muscle, wrapped in an amorous squeeze there, which serves as a kind of pump, and a restrainer. As she licks the edges of the dome now lifting her mouth completely up, air currents rush in, refreshingly stimulating; her hand continues to milk my *coc*, setting a pace, otherwise the explosion would come. She knows. She rests. I rest it, I open just the slits of my eyes to see that she has herself in a very relaxed position, so that she can last, without getting tired. I whisper the first words thick like *cum* in the air, "Baby, it's great, beautiful, oh I can't tell you how much—" But I don't finish, I feel her mouth's downward movement, engulfing the bulb as it relaxes from some of its previous excitement. She can detect its state by its throbbing, meaning to be very perfect, she eases the pressure of her hand, the cylinder somewhat dried where her hand has been pressed. I can even feel the sperm, free, push up, the quickening exit, though it is still very slow, still under her control, I am helpless. I am almost unconscious with the pleasure of it. She rotates her heated seminal-stained mouth five times swiftly on this meaty pendulous organ, *uume* . . .

Fighting my tendency to explode, she plans to shift the pace of her work, she uses no method for more than one second, for fear of tipping me off the delicate whimpering thin-skinned "construct" I'm being balanced on. She chews at it, with the gentle crunching of her teeth, tongue working, like she's chewing the juicy texture of an apple, she does this three times—it is so effective, so deeply sinewy good, closing distance between us, a kind of suspended liquid oneness holds us, I am in her, I am one, in her . . .

Then, quickly she suspends that game, and seems to be trying to "drink" it, like she'd drink water from a fountain in the park, a kind of sucking-up conflicting feeling, almost accommodating an earthquake of an orgasm!—that she restrains with a downward connective lapping of her tongue, gently taking up each drop of juice as it comes up out of the hot, irritated eye, the umbilical sweet, nexus-feeling of ME slowly being milked into her, slowly, she drinks ME, one drop, one rich corporeal swallow at a time. This is the only way to do it without having the orgasm so *powerful*, rushing up so swiftly that the action would be very painful, a struggle, all of it not being able to explode out the narrow head fast enough. She milks the tail, she goes very slowly, the harmony is perfect . . .

107

The symmetry of the way I'm coming is beautiful, this is the best I've ever had, the milking process she is using is a method she has perfected, developed on me (and probably on others I know nothing about), and it's great. With her mouth she fishes, ties knots with her tongue, around the bulb, she screws it as though she's using her pussy, she staples it quickly one or two times; then she rivets it, she hammers at it several times, she nails it down with stabs, it fights back in contraction, she puts a sash around it with her tongue, she seems to be padlocking it, linking it to her guts as she threatens to swallow it, the juices slowly draining out all along, the nexus deepening; now her mouth is thick with the creamy warm juice, slapping sounds of the pasty sperm from my swollen testicles, as the spermatic arteries are slowly being sweetly sucked up, slowly into this caramel beauty!

I will continue to come now until I am empty of semen, all of it that can come out, until my tubules are vacant, until the duct rests, without the nervous activity of excretion, I feel the careful building slim strength of her ligaments; now she seems to be throwing a lasso around my gun; suddenly she works it back toward herself, as though her mouth were reins, pulling at it, the spurts of semen thickening her pithy hole, still without hands; with her mouth she straightens it up, carefully, after swallowing most of the fluid, some of it sliding down the throbbing, nerve-racked pole still holding up in this phallus rite of sensuous music; and with it straight, she makes some sudden strokes that seem to be some kind of effort to bridle it like she might bridle a horse or a dog; the dick is kicking, slimy with sperm, throbbing nakedly buckling under so much tension, and she continues, keeping her grip just right, not finishing it; the juices continue to pour into her, she drinks them, and this is all done very slowly, now, with it standing nobly straight up again; her mouth seems to be working like ten busy fingers trying to button a button on a shirt, and my fluid is pumping up faster than ever—she detects this, puts her hands, both of them, on the upper part of the *kok*, and gently squeezes it as it bounces, punches, dribbles it around in her cave. She has relaxed her connection. She doesn't make a move with her mouth, the dick is swollen bigger than ever, resting, robust bulbous thing, throbbing, oozing smoothly, with restraint, into her, under this efficient "tongue-lashing," teasing, and mouthing. This edifice of mine, this lucky stretched-out time-space harmony, feels the comfort of her hand loosen, and the continuation of pleasant effusion. She is controlling this orgasm so well, it may go on for more than an hour, I am percolating, oozing, dribbling at the dick like a river, but a slow river, being tangled by the mysterious rainfalls of Mother, voids, secrets, wet holes of the flesh world, carrying on an expedition to the ends of my self-conscious reality; at the floodgates of emergency my dark, fleshy Anita, love, a gateway into which I exist, and erupt, enter; Oh! she frills it, gently, beginning again, now that the nerve-ends have stopped throbbing so . . .

She works at it like she's trimming corn off the cob, she skirts it, jerks it, confines it with quick frightening pressure, releases it, threads it, the juice gently secreting, Mr. Tail, ancient in his mighty moment; the sperm is just pouring out—but not the swift way it would in a normal explosive orgasm—as she nibbles at the edges of it, its prepuce slick with trimmings; the percolated head is so *swollen* the ejecting semen seems to feel choked in, but not painfully so, as it pushes, gushes, then trickles out, into her leaky hot mouth . . .

She ties a bowknot on it, making loud splash splash wet slappy sounds, zips up and down up down up down (faster than ever—) on the final up, grabs the head of the cable meat, squares it in her nest, locks it tightly, juices splashing, jumping, buckling into her thicker, hotter than ever, rich, oozing circuits of seedy fluid jamming into her; she takes them without blinking, still anchoring the dicker connectively, roped to her control, not allowed to empty, finish completely until she says so . . .

Huge emotional collisions in me, I had no idea I could ever generate so much fluid at one time. The padlock of her mouth now merely restrains it, but loosely, as she steadily holds it; it is like a wet electric meat god, cabling magic into her, screwing the tunnel of us close, stopping up the ends, to make us one rope.

I feel now the shift of her body. She adjusts herself for the Big Moment. She has planned to bring me into the finish. She is going to work it very carefully, make its *interconnection* so well bridged, so rich, *free low flowing*, consistent, to make it so complete and agreeable, tunneling into her, the flowing upbeat of the incessant cargo of fluid that completes the symphony. She is getting ready to start. I try not to brace myself.

I succeed in remaining as relaxed as I am, my wet *cokke*

though has the sharp knowledge conveyed to it, and it stiffens, hard as a tendon, its prepuce slimy as the slick spongy head: I feel the top of her mouth slowly sinking down to rest on the protuberance of it. How do I know she is ready? She takes both my balls in one hand, and holds gently the belly of them but firmly, while they pout, my extremely bloated peninsula of a dickhead thickly tightens, "feeling" *her readiness* to work at it. She begins! She really goes! Until every drop of it is *gushing* out.

WHAM! down she comes, *zipping.* the antagonistic wet grip of her contracting expanding mouth is sucking, fucking it, chewing it, UP–DOWN! updown! . . . The dick is so shocked it stops even the slow corporeal leakage, stunned. But quickly the "shape" of it circles in, the magic excitement increases during this wild, twisting, collapsing moment my dingdong begins to spit up semen again, responding to it—this *overwhelming impact,* this squeezing, sucking, and I hear the sloppy juices jumping, splashing around in her mouth; she is holding my balls and milking them of their substance, milking and milking, and *pumping,* jacking, fucking my cock with all she has, the contour of its working shapes against the round surface of my meat god, sucking him, sucking him, getting him UP, up—inelastic rootdepth throbbings, I am almost out, with the rushing—pushing feelings pouring up out of me, up into her, bursting, *blind unconscious* (too much trying to come out at once)— She holds the balls, understanding what is happening, bringing modified rivers of seed out of my loins! She still controls his ebb, as she pumps—*now now now blindly dead blind sweet sweeeeetly oh,*

111

and I do groan, even shriek, this bonanza is so rich, it is *bursting*—
My senses stewing, fermented, quivering—I am breathless, unable to move, as she has it all out except for the last few drops,
she hungrily sucks—

*Oh how beautiful gentle she is* with it as she licks it, the yeasty
last drops, the end of the turmoil, how she mothers it, holds my
stomach just above the line of my hair for a moment, then takes
prepuce with the other hand and holding just the head of this
cherry-tipped, sore, nerve-wracked but happy *kok* pushes it back
from the inhabitant beneath it, still throbbing, as he shrinks only
theoretically, not actually, still too *tense:* he will stay hard, though
empty, for a while yet; now, she gently sucks at it, like she's eating
plums, pulling off the skins, and this brings out the tiniest of the
tiny last drops of semen, the juices, and to make sure she has it all
out, so that I am completely happy, she softly, rhythmically, mas-
turbates it slowly; this is too taxing, the *pain* of it, I have to grip her
hand, and stop her . . .

So, she knows she's done a beautiful job, and I try to open
one eye enough to see her, and when I manage it, she's there, in
the yellow light, big, soft red lips as she wipes them with the edge
of the sheet, smelling spermy, and looking naked and ripe as a
peach, and now I'm ready.

### ᵈ❡ PAULE MARSHALL ❡ᵇ

# Praisesong for the Widow

*Paule Marshall's parents emigrated from Barbados to New York during World War I. She was born in 1929 and grew up in Brooklyn during the Depression. She graduated Phi Beta Kappa from Brooklyn College in 1953. Her works include* Brown Girl, Brownstones; Soul Clap Hands and Sing; The Chosen Place, The Timeless People; *and* Praisesong for the Widow. *I chose this excerpt because, although not explicitly sexual, it is extremely sensual and beautifully written.*

SHE WENT ABOUT THE BATH WITH GREAT DISCRETION. WHILE Avey Johnson kept her eyes closed she first meticulously washed her face and neck, soaping, rinsing, drying them, her touch light and impersonal. Only when this was done did she remove the nightgown—and she managed to slip it off without scarcely disturbing the sheet covering her. From then on she took care to turn back the sheet only enough to expose the limb or place she was washing at the moment. And whenever Avey Johnson flinched or stiffened involuntarily, she would stop, give the towel or washcloth to the maid to hold, and bring her hands to rest quietly on her for a minute or two before continuing.

Slowly, in a manner designed to put Avey Johnson at ease, she washed a hand, an arm, a shoulder, a breast, bathing only one side of her at a time which made it easier to keep her covered. When, after some time, she reached the emptied-out plain of her stomach and her pelvis below she did not turn or fold back the sheet, but simply held it up slightly with one hand so that it formed a low canopy as she thoroughly washed her there.

Her long legs came next, and then Rosalie Parvay, followed by the maid bearing the washtub, was moving around to the other side of the bed.

For a long while there was silence in the room. As if the bath was an office they performed every day for some stranger passing through, Rosalie Parvay and the maid smoothly exchanged the washcloth, towels and soap between them without uttering a word. The younger woman, her face closed and expressionless under her white cap, did not budge from beside the washtub. Nor did she speak the whole time she was in the room.

Rosalie Parvay also remained silent. With her sharply planed, thin-lipped face she quietly and with great tact went about the bath, her earring glinting against her blackness whenever she turned to signal the maid, the peaks on her headtie probing the air like antennae. Until finally, as she was washing the other shoulder, her lips began to move, and the silence was broken by what sounded like a plainsong or a chant—a long string of half-spoken, half-sung words in Patois. It was a curious, scarcely audible singsong, addressed neither to the maid nor to Avey Johnson. And it was to go on for the rest of the bath, without once charging inflection or tone.

Gradually, under Rosalie Parvay's discreet touch and the welcome feel of the soap and water on her skin, Avey Johnson had found herself growing less opposed to being bathed. Now there was the hushed singsong voice in the room, and this also helped ease her tension. So that by the time, halfway through the bath, when Rosalie Parvay briefly interrupted herself to ask her to turn over to have her back washed, she had come to accept and even to enjoy somewhat the feel of the small expert hands on her body.

She gave herself over then to the musing voice and to such simple matters as the mild fragrance of the soap on the air and the lovely sound, like a sudden light spatter of rain, as the maid wrung out the washcloth from time to time over the water in the galvanized tub.

Hadn't there been a tub like it out in back of the house in Tatem? It suddenly came to her that there had been—another memory drifting up out of the void. One the same size even, and with the same three or four grooves by way of decoration running around the top that she had glimpsed on the washtub here before Rosalie Parvay had closed her eyes. And the same dull gray in color. It had been her bathtub during those August visits. While her great-aunt rigorously administered the weekly scrubbing, she would sit drawn up in the tub, picking the patches of sunlight from the live oak tree overhead off her knees and blowing them like soap bubbles or thistledown into the air.

The memory took over, and for long minutes she was the child in the washtub again.

Limes. The faint cool smell of limes on the air brought her back to the room, and her eyes opening, looking—questioning— over her shoulder, she discovered Rosalie Parvay, the bath finished at last, gently rubbing her back with a lime-scented oil from a bottle the maid was holding.

The instant her eyes opened, the small hand immediately went up to silence any protest she might have. "Is only a little light oil, oui, to see to it your skin don' get dry. I gon' be finish just now."

With that said the hand dropped, and on its way down, it touched Avey Johnson's eyes, closing them for the second time, and taking up her speechlike song again, Rosalie Parvay finished oiling her back before asking her to turn over.

She went about this phase of the bath with the same discretion as before, folding back the sheet only as much as necessary as she slowly made her way around the bed again, with the silent maid in attendance at her elbow. From time to time uncorking the bottle in her hand the younger woman shook a drop or two of the oil into Rosalie Parvay's outstretched palm, and without being asked she occasionally passed her mistress a hand towel she had draped over her arm for her to wipe the perspiration from her forehead—the two of them joined in a single rhythm which made it seem that the rubdown, like the bath, was something they were long used to doing.

And Rosalie Parvay wasn't content just to oil Avey Johnson's body. She was also lightly kneading the flesh across her shoulders and down her back and sides between her small hands. And when she turned to the limbs—which came in for most of her attention—she not only oiled and kneaded them thoroughly, but afterwards proceeded to stretch them by repeatedly running her hands down from a shoulder to a wrist or from a knee to an ankle, gently yet firmly pulling and stretching the limb before she finally drew back and covered it again with the sheet.

It was the way Avey Johnson used to stretch the limbs of her children after giving them their baths when they were infants. To see to it that their bones grew straight. Putting them to lie on the kitchen table in Halsey Street, she would first rub them down with the baby oil, and afterwards taking each puffy little arm in her hands, then the legs that were still partly curled to fit inside her, she would repeatedly stroke and pull on them in the same gentle yet firm manner—stretching, straightening the small limbs. At the end, grasping them by the ankles, she would dangle them briefly head down, then hold them high in the air for a second by the wrists as if to show off their perfection to the world.

Meanwhile, Rosalie Parvay had turned her attention to the upper half of her legs which she had left for the last. And her touch, Avey Johnson realized, her body stiffening momentarily, had changed. As if challenged by the sight of the flesh there, which had grown thick and inert from years of the long-line girdle, she was vigorously kneading it between hands that felt as strong suddenly as the maid's beside her looked to be.

And she was utterly concentrated. Her little ruminative singsong died. She ceased using the oil, so that Avey Johnson, who

117

knew it was futile to protest, felt the roughness of her small palms along the entire length of her thighs. And when the maid reached over from time to time to offer her the towel she took no notice. She was oblivious to everything but the sluggish flesh she was working between her hands as if it were the dough of the bread she had baked that morning or clay that had yet to be shaped and fired.

Until finally under the vigorous kneading and pummeling, Avey Johnson became aware of a faint stinging as happens in a limb that's fallen asleep once it's roused, and a warmth could be felt as if the blood there had been at a standstill, but was now tentatively getting under way again. And this warmth and the faint stinging reached up the entire length of her thighs. (Their length and shapeliness would excite him even when she was dressed and he couldn't see them, Jay, talking his talk, used to say.) Then, slowly, they radiated out into her loins: When, when was the last time she had felt even the slightest stirring there? (Just take it from me! Jerome Johnson used to say.) The warmth, the stinging sensation that was both pleasure and pain passed up through the emptiness at her center. Until finally they reached her heart. And as they encircled her heart and it responded, there was the sense of a chord being struck. All the tendons, nerves and muscles, which strung her together had been struck a powerful chord, and the reverberation could be heard in the remotest corners of her body.

◁| BERNICE L. McFADDEN |▷

# Sugar

*Bernice L. McFadden is deeply rooted in the familial oral histories of the South. Her first novel, Sugar, was widely praised. She is currently living in Brooklyn and working on her next book. This excerpt, one of my favorites, is an extremely sensual description of a woman naked, alone, exposing herself to the night.*

PEARL SAT ON HER BED STARING AT THE FLOOR. PERIODICALLY she would look over at the worn Bible that sat conspicuously on the nightstand beside the bed. Its black cracked cover seemed to fill the whole room and dwarf her. There was nothing in the Bible that said you shouldn't dye your hair. There were no words that said, Thou shalt not befriend a whore. No, Pearl knew the Bible from cover to cover, and those shalt not's did not exist.

Pearl got up and went to the full-length mirror that stood in the corner of her room. She stood before it and looked at herself, the new her. She fingered her hair, soft, silky and black. She touched her face, ran her fingers over the face that was absent of wrinkles. Her eyes held her age, not the skin on her face. Slowly, methodically, without being totally conscious of her movements, she began to disrobe. She slipped her dress over her head. The slip followed, as did the brassiere and stockings and panties. She stood before herself, her naked self, and began to re-familiarize herself with her body.

The once flat stomach was rounded and protruded forward; it was scarred with motherhood marks three times over. If she could, she would not even sell those long, black marks that criss-crossed her abdomen, no, they made up who she was—a mother.

The breasts that once sat high and curved now sloped, but did not sag. Her hips were thicker, rounder, and so were her legs. She turned to examine her behind. It was large, expanded by time and good eating. All in all, Pearl did not have a body unworthy of wanting. She released the French roll and let her hair cascade down onto her shoulders. Wild, black waves of hair. She giggled to herself and hurriedly covered her mouth with her hands.

The night was dawning dark blue as the full moon took its place high above Bigelow, giving light to dark back roads and lost souls. A breeze kicked up, late-night September air that pre-pared you for October and beyond moved through the open window, provoking the curtains into shrill and frenzied move-ments. Without thinking, Pearl moved to close the window, and in doing so, exposed herself to the night. She stopped, but did not draw back. The night air moved seductively across her naked body. It was tantalizing and invigorating. Slowly, the night caressed her, transforming her nipples into resistant pebbles and teasing the small, pointed, pink flesh between her legs. Pearl parted the curtains and leaned the top part of her body out of the window, allowing her breasts to sway slowly in the night air. The night welcomed her nakedness. It felt so good, so right, so free. Suddenly, she understood.

This sudden empathy she felt for Sugar sent her reeling back from the open window. She snatched her clothes up from the floor and wrapped them, best she could, around her nakedness. What was she if she was able to take part in, understand and even enjoy an act that was clearly amoral? Had her acceptance of Sugar made her susceptible to her low-down traits? Was being a whore like having a flu—could you catch it like the diseases that hid and floated invisible in the air? A shaken, unsure laugh bounced off the walls. "I'm being so stupid," Pearl said aloud and dropped her clothes back down to the floor. She started toward the closet door to retrieve her gown from the hook it hung on during the day. As she went, she caught, once again, the naked sight of herself in the mirror and something in her smiled.

## ⊰ TONI MORRISON ⊱

# Jazz

*Toni Morrison was born in Lorain, Ohio, and educated at Howard University and Cornell. She has written eight critically acclaimed novels:* The Bluest Eye; Sula; Song of Solomon, *which won the 1978 National Book Critics Circle Award;* Tar Baby; Beloved, *which won the 1998 Pulitzer Prize;* Jazz; Paradise; *and* Love. *She was awarded the Nobel Prize for literature in 1993. She is the Robert F. Goheen Professor, Council of the Humanities, Princeton University. Of all her scenes regarding intimacy, I chose this one for its joy and tenderness.*

THERE WAS AN EVENING, BACK IN 1906, BEFORE JOE AND VIOLET went to the City, when Violet left the plow and walked into their little shotgun house, the heat of the day still stunning. She was wearing coveralls and a sleeveless faded shirt and slowly removed them along with the cloth from her head. On a table near the cookstove stood an enamel basin—speckled blue and white and chipped all round its rim. Under a square of toweling, placed there to keep insects out, the basin was full of still water. Palms up, fingers leading, Violet slid her hands into the water and rinsed her face. Several times she scooped and splashed until, perspiration and water mixed, her cheeks and forehead cooled. Then, dipping the toweling into the water, carefully she bathed. From the windowsill she took a white shift, laundered that very morning, and dropped it over her head and shoulders. Finally she sat on the bed to unwind her hair. Most of the knots fixed that morning had loosened under her headcloth and were now cupfuls of soft wool her fingers thrilled to. Sitting there, her hands deep in the forbidden pleasure of her hair, she noticed she had not removed her heavy work shoes. Putting the toe of her left foot to the heel of the right, she pushed the shoe off. The effort seemed extra and the mild surprise at how very tired she felt was interrupted by a soft, wide hat, as worn and dim as the room she sat in, descending on her. Violet did not feel her shoulder touch the mattress. Way before that she had entered a safe sleep. Deep, trustworthy, feathered in colored dreams. The heat was relentless, insinuating. Like the voices of the women in houses nearby singing "Go down, go down, way down in Egypt land . . ." Answering each other from yard to yard with a verse or its variation.

Joe had been away for two months at Crossland, and when he got home and stood in the doorway, he saw Violet's dark girl-body limp on the bed. She looked frail to him, and penetrable everyplace except at one foot, the left, where her man's work shoe remained. Smiling, he took off his straw hat and sat down at the bottom of the bed. One of her hands held her face; the other rested on her thigh. He looked at the fingernails hard as her palm skin, and noticed for the first time how shapely her hands were. The arm that curved out of the shift's white sleeve was muscled by field labor, awful thin, but smooth as a child's. He undid the laces of her shoe and eased it off. It must have helped something in her dream for she laughed then, a light happy laugh that he had never heard before, but which seemed to belong to her.

◄§| ALBERT MURRAY |§►

# The Seven League Boots

*Albert Murray was born in Nokomis, Alabama, and educated at Tuskegee Institute, where he later taught literature and theatre. A retired major in the United States Air Force, he has written many works of fiction and nonfiction including an autobiography,* South to a Very Old Place, *and the novels* Train Whistle Guitar, The Spyglass Tree, *and* Seven League Boots. *He lives in New York City.*

WHEN SHE CAME BACK DOWNSTAIRS WEARING A PALE BLUE SILK smock with off-white raw silk slacks and patent leather flats, she had also combed her hair so that it was shoulder length, and she looked more like the famous screen and fan magazine personality than the no less glamorous but somehow somewhat less familiar woman who had just brought me home with her.

The woman I had met less than an hour ago outside the Keynote had in effect been a familiar all but improbably friendly stranger with whom I had instantly become involved in a very cordial person-to-person relationship that was as yet undefined. Now suddenly she was the Jewel Templeton you had come to know so intimately from all of the closer-than-life closeups, special camera angles, and sound effects that you felt that you could not only read the way her eyes and lips and nostrils reacted in a whole range of intimate situations but also how her breath already sounded before the words came.

She put her empty glass on the serving cart and stood with her left hand behind her neck, her cheek against her forearm, her hair falling around her raised elbow; and when she saw that I was following my shot of bourbon with a tall glass of seltzer she helped herself to the same, and after her second sip she said, Oh say, if you worked from the first set you've not had anything to eat since lunchtime, or midafternoon at the latest. So how about something to eat? And suddenly remembering that all I had eaten since breakfast was a hamburger with a vanilla malted in the midafternoon I said, Well, now that you bring it up.

Which was when she slapped her forehead and said, Oh my God, there is dinner! I had completely forgotten all about it. Now that's really something, I mean really. You have no idea. Not that I have a huge appetite. But mealtime is not something that often skips my mind. Unless I'm deeply absorbed in some special undertaking. So I guess I must be even more excited about all this than I realized.

The help had left at six, she told me as she beckoned for me to follow her up to the dining area, where she set two plates, but except for a few little personal finishing touches that she always insisted on adding, everything was ready and waiting.

Then I also followed along as she went on into the kitchen, and when she saw how curious I was about all of the special equipment and utensils, she said, I have accumulated all these fancy gadgets because I myself am something of a fancy cook. You have no idea what a special thing this food thing is with me, in spite of all the concern about staying thin that the mere mention of Hollywood brings to mind. I actually designed this kitchen along with my first husband, who as you probably know was a set designer and also something of an architect—or in any case a collaborating architect.

As for the size of the kitchen library, she had been given her first guide to French food and a handbook of French wines in preparation for her first trip to Europe when she was eighteen and had begun adding new and old titles before the trip was over, and before long food and wine books had become a very special enthusiasm. Her taste was basically French, but she also was almost as taken with Italian cuisine, and then came German, Polish, Scandinavian, and other European dishes; and her menu might include Spanish, Portuguese, and Latin American specialties any day of the week.

Not unlike many other people along the Pacific Coast she also ate a lot of Polynesian, Chinese, and Japanese food, but with so many outstanding Far Eastern restaurants and caterers so readily available, she had never felt the urge to try out any Far Eastern recipes at home except when among the gift packages that she received from fans from many lands there were Far Eastern food items with recipes included.

Among her special food loving friends there were, to be sure, also a number of winemakers, those in France and Italy predating those in northern California, who had in due course come to out-number them by a considerable margin. Some of these also be-longed to a special circle of "mushroom friends," many of whom also grew their own herbs and spices.

The main dish that night was neither strictly French nor Ital-ian. She called it Escallops in Short Order and explained each step as she zipped along. The pieces of veal were already cut and dusted in flour so all she had to do was sauté them quickly in olive oil and splash in the right amount of dry vermouth and beef stock, let the gravy thicken slightly, and then sprinkle in already prepared fresh rosemary, chopped scallion, and parsley and wafer thin slices of lemon. And *voilà*, in less time than it took to play through three selections of approximately three minutes each.

She made a salad dressing of olive oil, fresh lemon juice, and sea salt in which she tossed Bibb lettuce and sliced plum toma-toes in a wooden bowl rubbed with a half clove of garlic. She said that there was a choice of a red wine, a chilled white wine, or both but that the red would go better with the cheese course. So that's how I came to have my first taste of Barolo and the cheese was gorgonzola and for bread you had a choice of crusty French or Italian rolls or you could either cut or break the French ficelles to suit yourself.

Meanwhile the records I had chosen included "Six Twenty-seven Stomp" (as in Musicians Local 627), with Pete Johnson on piano with a seven-piece group of Kansas City all stars; "Piney Brown Blues," with Joe Turner singing along with Pete Johnson and several of the same all stars; "Baby Dear" and "Harmony Blues," with Mary Lou Williams on piano with her Kansas City Seven (from Andy Kirk's band); "The Count" and "Twelfth Street Rag" by Andy Kirk and the Twelve Clouds of Joy, with Mary Lou Williams on piano; "Good Morning Blues" (with Jimmy Rushing on vocal) and "Doggin' Around" by Count Basie; and "Moten Swing" and "I Want a Little Girl" by a group led by Eddie Durham, trombone player, a pioneer electric guitar player and key arranger for the late Bennie Moten and the early Count Basie orchestra.

We skipped dessert and coffee and brought the leftover wine back to the main part of the drawing room, where she curled up in what was obviously her favorite overstuffed chair and I took over the operation of the sound system; and when I said, You can go either way from Kansas City, south to the blues and New Orleans and Louis Armstrong and all of that, or east to stride time in Harlem and Duke Ellington and all of that, she said, Whatever you say, maestro. So I said, Why don't we just stick with what we already have going? And she said, Why don't we indeed?

Then she also said, May I take that to mean that you approve of what you have found so far? And when I said, No question about it and said, I can't get over finding so much of this stuff up here in these elegant hills, that was when she told me that she had been shopping from a list prepared for her by a newfound friend in St. Moritz last winter.

Believe it or not, she said, that was really the first time I ever stopped and listened to the blues as you listen to what is called serious music. I must tell you all about that because that is really what all this goes back to: the Marquis de Chaumienne, my favorite twentieth-century human being. He is an extremely handsome sixty-seven-year-old French diplomat, sportsman, and patron of the arts, whose family involvement with America goes all the way back to the time of De Tocqueville, and whose knowledge of the things that make America American is absolutely staggering, especially to somebody with my conventional midwestern upbringing.

Oh I really must tell you about what happened when I finally got to meet and become friends with him over there last winter. I most definitely must and now that I think of it, I can hardly wait. But not tonight. He himself would not have me interrupt this music for that.

So we went on playing the records I had set aside. And in answer to questions that she would signal for a pause to ask from time to time, I said what I said about the infinite flexibility of Kansas City four/four, riffs, and riff chorus compositions, about stomps, jumps, and shouts, about voicings, timbre, mutes, plungers, aluminum, plastic, and felt derbies and also about how the old Kansas City jam sessions were said to be similar to and different from the ones in the Keynote.

Then to call attention to how late it was getting to be I said, And now for an example or so of the after hours groove if the time will allow. And she said, Oh by all means. And when I began with Count Basie on piano with his rhythm section of

Walter Page on bass, Jo Jones on drums, and Freddie Green on guitar playing "The Dirty Dozen" from the stack that also included "How Long Blues," "The Fives," "Hey Lordy, Mama" "Boogie-Woogie" and "Oh Red," and she said, Perfect, just simply precious. I can't wait to tell the marquis about this. Oh I don't believe this really.

Your choices are among his favorite examples of what he calls the functional and therefore truly authentic American chamber music, she said. According to the marquis, whose explorations in the United States also included the back alley honky-tonks, jook joints, and barrelhouses, it was in the gin mills, cocktail lounges, and small intimate after hours hole-in-the-wall joints that you found the twentieth-century equivalent to the music you heard in the elegant European chambers of the old castles and châteaus of yesteryear.

She stood up and began moving around the room doing dance studio warmup stretches and she dimmed the lights. Then when I put the Eddie Durham octet version of "Moten Swing" on again, she came striding back in my direction with her back ever so statuesque, her shoulders square, her legs and thighs moving like a Busby Berkeley chorus girl and I began snapping my fingers and tilting my head on the diagonal.

We were facing each other like that for the first time then, and as she opened her arms she also stepped out of her flats saying, Do you know what this shoe thing is about? And when I said, What kind of old shoe thing? she said, This barefoot thing some of us have. There's supposed to be some big symbolic something about it. There are these friends of mine who insist that there is something about this kind of music that all but literally undresses them, that makes them respond as if they are or should be naked.

◂[ GLORIA NAYLOR ]▸

# The Women of Brewster Place

*Gloria Naylor is a New Yorker born and raised. She received her B.A. in English from Brooklyn College and her M.A. in Afro-American Studies from Yale.* The Women of Brewster Place, *her hugely popular debut novel, won the American Book Award for first fiction in 1983.*

HE TOOK HER ARM AND HELPED HER INTO THE FRONT SEAT OF HIS car. Her back sank into the deep upholstered leather, and the smell of the freshly vacuumed carpet was mellow in her nostrils. All of the natural night sounds of the city were blocked by the thick tinted windows and the hum of the air conditioner, but they trailed persistently behind the polished back of the vehicle as it turned and headed down the long gray boulevard.

> *Smooth road*
> *Clear day*
> *But why am I the only one*
> *Traveling this way*

*How strange the road to love*
*Can be so easy*
*Can there be a detour ahead?*

Moreland Woods was captivated by the beautiful woman at his side. Her firm brown flesh and bright eyes carried the essence of nectar from some untamed exotic flower, and the fragrance was causing a pleasant disturbance at the pit of his stomach. He marveled at how excellently she played the game. A less alert observer might have been taken in, but his survival depended upon knowing people, knowing exactly how much to give and how little to take. It was this razor-thin instinct that had catapulted him to the head of his profession and that would keep him there.

And although she cut her cards with a reckless confidence, pushed her chips into the middle of the table as though the supply was unlimited, and could sit out the game until dawn, he knew. Oh, yes. Let her win a few, and then he would win just a few more, and she would be bankrupt long before the sun was up. And then there would be only one thing left to place on the table—and she would, because the stakes they were playing for were very high. But she was going to lose that last deal. She would lose because when she first sat down in that car she had everything riding on the fact that he didn't know the game existed.

And so it went. All evening Etta had been in another world, weaving his tailored suit and the smell of his expensive cologne into a custom-made future for herself. It took his last floundering thrusts into her body to bring her back to reality. She arrived in enough time to feel him beating against her like a dying walrus, until he shuddered and was still.

She kept her eyes closed because she knew when she opened them there would be the old familiar sights around her. To her right would be the plastic-coated nightstand that matched the cheaply carved headboard of the bed she lay in. She felt the bleached coarseness of the sheet under her sweaty back and predicted the roughness of the worn carpet path that led from the bed to the white-tiled bathroom with bright fluorescent lights, sterilized towels, and tissue-wrapped water glasses. There would be two or three small thin rectangles of soap wrapped in bright waxy covers that bore the name of the hotel.

She didn't try to visualize what the name would be. It didn't matter. They were all the same, all meshed together into one lump that rested like an iron ball on her chest. And the expression on the face of this breathing mass to her left would be the same as all the others. She could turn now and go through the rituals that would tie up the evening for them both, but she wanted just one more second of this soothing darkness before she had to face the echoes of the locking doors she knew would be in his eyes.

# It Begins with Tears

*Opal Palmer Adisa was born in Kingston, Jamaica, moved to New York to study at Hunter College, and returned to Jamaica to write and direct radio programs for children. Her poetry, short stories, and articles have appeared in numerous anthologies. Her works include* The Many-Eyed Fruit, Bake-Face and Other Guava Stories, *and* Tamarind and Mango Women. *She currently lives in California with her three children.*

ABOUT A WEEK LATER NATHAN STARTED COMING ROUND IN THE evenings after he finished his trade, and the dressmaker remarked that he might make some smart woman a good husband as carpenters could make lots of money, if only he learned to wash his underarms more thoroughly and put on some deodorant. 'Is not jungle we live in any more, you know. You would tink a nice man like Nathan would rub some deodorant under his arms,' she lamented.

Arnella winced, remembering the first time Nathan awkwardly touched her. Sandpaper was smoother than his palm, she was certain. She told him he should rub coconut oil on his palms every night, and he must have taken her advice, for several months later when he tentatively placed his hand on her arm, it felt smoother. Still, she could not bear his touch. She liked him, but not enough to encourage his advances. Throughout the three years of her apprenticeship Arnella saw Nathan often, but as a friend. She got to see more of his work in other people's homes, when she went to deliver their dresses. Also, the dressmaker had commissioned several pieces from him. Although Arnella had always assumed that Godfree would make all her furniture, after seeing Nathan's work she decided to ask him to make her a bed. She knew exactly the bed she wanted, having looked at many in books from abroad and in the furniture stores around town. But Nathan refused to look at any of the pictures she tried to show him, nor would he listen to Arnella's ideas about design. 'Ah gwane mek you a bed you gwane love,' he had insisted, and refused to hear any more about it. Arnella was doubtful, but decided that if she didn't like it she could give it to Velma.

Several months went by and Arnella prepared to leave her apprenticeship and assist another dressmaker on St James Street in Montego Bay. She had seen Nathan several times, but he had said nothing about her bed. Two more months after her move Arnella asked Nathan if he would soon be finished with her bed, but he merely said, 'Hold tight, mon. When it done, you de first to see it.' So Arnella decided never to mention the bed again. Besides, she didn't have her own place. Where would she put a bed anyway?

On a Saturday morning, almost a year to the day Arnella had asked Nathan to make the bed, he came by the dressmaking shop on St James Street. He said he had something to show her. Arnella couldn't imagine what it could be, but she saw he was wearing a clean yellow shirt that opened at the neck and illuminated his skin, and grey pants, with shoes that were clean and newlooking. Curious, and encouraged by his smile and his smart attire, Arnella agreed at last to go with him. They walked along beside each other and from time to time their hands brushed, but Arnella pulled quickly away, making a space between them.

After leading her down many streets, Nathan turned into a lane that smelled of urine and whose gutters were clogged with rubbish. Arnella pinched her nose to keep out the smell. Midway down the lane, Nathan turned and entered a yard. A brown mutt ran up and rubbed against his legs, then went back to lie under the straggly soursop tree in the smooth, dirt-swept yard. Nathan led Arnella to a large barn-like door which he opened slowly, saying as he nudged her in, 'Dis is fi me workshop.' Arnella looked around at the yard, devoid of life except for the brown mutt; she hesitated, unsure. Then, glancing at Nathan and reassured by his warm look, she entered slowly. Her eyes adjusted to the dark interior. The smell of sawdust and furniture stain tickled her nose and she sneezed. 'Guzzum!' Nathan said at her back. She felt him close behind her, and was about to accuse him. But then she saw it, directly in front of her, and knew it was her bed. Her mouth fell open but she covered it with her hands. Her eyes glittered, and she spun first to stare wide-eyed at Nathan, then back to get a closer look at the bed-head. Two diamond-shaped mirrors were embedded at each end of the frame. At the centre of the frame were carved a man, a woman and a row of children holding hands, stretching across the entire frame and seeming to disappear into the mirrors at both ends. Then, built to create a shelf effect, were a woman's breasts.

Arnella felt sweat forming at her armpits. She folded her arms across her chest and caressed her elbows. Nathan pulled the base of the bed into the shaft of light that stole through the open door. Laughter sputtered from Arnella's lips, and she bit back her excitement. The base of the bed was in the voluptuous form of a woman's bottom. It appeared as if beads were roped around the woman's waist and came to rest on her high behind. Arnella felt suddenly weak and would have lain down if there had been a mattress. Luckily there wasn't. She kneeled and sniffed at the wood, like a dog in search of a tree. Her hands lingered over the wood, the tips of her fingers tenderly circling the grains and crevices. She moved to touch the bed frame, and that was when she noticed the two built-in drawers, on which was carved the upper half of a woman's body, her head in profile, her hands raised gracefully above her head with arms and fingers curled like a dancer.

Arnella was speechless. She had never imagined anything so beautiful. She was reluctant to turn round and face Nathan because she had never suspected such depths of talent or beauty resided within him. But as this realisation came to her, she was struck by sudden apprehension. She couldn't afford this bed. Surely Nathan hadn't made something so incredible just to give it away. Arnella swallowed and faced him.

'Is how me gwane pay you for dis?'

'You like it?'

'How you mean if me like it? Lawd God, Nathan, it nuff pretty. It beautiful. Is a work of art!'

Nathan beamed and his hands in his pockets trembled. This was her bed. He had made it for her and she wanted it. Perhaps at last he would sleep with her. But Arnella would not lead him on any more. Nathan was an artist and deserved her honesty. She liked him a lot, but still felt no desire to have him kiss her or to be his girl. She wished she did, so she could thank him, but honesty was all the thanks she had for him.

Nathan didn't say anything when she said, 'Nathan, it no mek sense you wasting you time. Nice man like you can find a good woman fi love him.' Nathan only looked at the ground and kicked the sawdust with his feet. After a lengthy silence, with their breathing sounding out a rhythm, Nathan finally said, 'Come mek me walk you back.' Arnella walked out into the light ahead of Nathan, and waited by the gate while he padlocked his workshop. The walk back to St James Street was long. Arnella and Nathan walked like perfect strangers, and if someone had been watching them, she would have been surprised when Nathan stopped the ice-cream man riding past them on his bicycle cart and bought Arnella a chocolate fudge. When they got to the gate of the yard in which Arnella now lived and worked,

Nathan took her hands in his rough, large palms, rubbed them, then walked off, his head searching the ground. Mid-way in the block, he threw over his shoulder, 'Ah will keep de bed till you ready fah it.'

◀ GWENDOLYN M. PARKER ▶

# These Same Long Bones

*Born in North Carolina and educated at Radcliffe, Gwendolyn M. Parker gave up her extremely lucrative career as an international tax attorney and marketing manager on Wall Street to devote herself to writing full time. She is the author of the novel* These Same Long Bones. *She currently lives in Connecticut.*

"AILIE," SIRUS SAID, BUT AILEEN DIDN'T HEAR HIM. HE TRIED gently to pull her hands away from her face, and then tried to move her legs from her chest, but Aileen resisted, and as he tried harder, she pulled herself tighter. So they stayed like that, their tensions and strengths equal, neither moving, until Sirus took his hands away and let them hover above her, stroking the space between them. He poured all of his love into that space, using everything these painful days had forced him to know, and he circled her around with his love, which was open to heartache, and cruelty, even death, stroking the air between them, around and around, slowly, ever so slowly, closer and closer, until just his fingers brushed her skin, feathering across her. He trailed one finger slowly after the other, and soon, as she let him, his touch grew a little stronger, so that he was stroking her, then kneading her skin, then taking her face in his hands. He cupped his hands over hers on her face.

"Ailie, look at me," he said.

She let her hands drop and slowly looked up. In her husband's face she recognized the child they had birthed together and had lost.

"You're so soft," she said, and as she said it, she suddenly knew it was true. As she looked at him, she saw, as if she had never seen him before, that he was as soft as she was, not at all strong the way she'd always imagined, but soft at the center, soft at the center of his eyes, at the center of his heart, where anything and everything could pierce him, just as things pierced her, and his strength was just muscle and bone that shielded his soft heart.

"Hold me," she said, and Sirus took her into his arms. He held her against his chest, where she could hear his heart beating, and she wrapped her arms around his chest and up to where she could stroke his face. She could feel the pulse behind his ear and he could feel her breasts against him and she could feel his breath in her hair and he could feel her eyelids moving across his chest. They held on to each other, each melting into the other, all the grief and the anger and the reserve and the guilt melting, until there was nothing left in either of them but a hole into which they were both opening.

"You loved our child, Ailie," Sirus said.

Neither of them moved. They kept their arms tight around each other until the sun came up, each falling slowly, deeper and deeper, closer and closer to the center of the other's heart.

◄| CARYL PHILLIPS |►

# Higher Ground

*Caryl Phillips was born in 1958 in St. Kitts, West Indies, and came with his family to England later that same year. He grew up in Leeds and was educated at Oxford. He is a prolific scriptwriter for film, theater, radio, and television, as well as a highly acclaimed novelist whose work includes* The Final Passage, Higher Ground, Cambridge, *and* Crossing the River.

PERHAPS THE SOLDIERS ARE BEGINNING TO NOTICE THAT I AM
re food than is normal. I do not mind so long as
pect the real reason behind my excessive ap-
again, how could they? I take few chances. She
t night for a breath of fresh air; the rest of the
n my quarters. I bring her water and food; I at-
and talk with her. And, of course, I make her,
s side of our relationship problematic for I as-
sociate our love-play with guilt. I worry that perhaps I undertake
such risks for mere physical gratification. I worry that she feels
this, but we do not speak of it. I break a crust of bread and give
the larger piece to her. 'Your father is the Head Man in your

village?' I repeat the information, unable to believe that he could have treated his own daughter in this way. She looks at me and shrugs. 'As soon as the man chose me I was tainted. My father had to disown me. Have you already forgotten the ways of your own people?' I take the rebuke with a straight face, for in it there is an element of truth. There are many things about our people that I have forgotten. She causes me to remember. 'And it was only a matter of chance that he chose you on the day you lined up with the others?' She laughs. 'Of course it was chance. Do you think I wanted to go from my family into the arms of such a man? As he pointed towards me my life was over.' She stops. 'But you did nothing to help me and I hated you for that.' I feel I have to explain. I stand and walk away from her. She lies on the bed of straw. She has encouraged my wounds to heal and once again I feel whole. I walk with conviction. She would have made an outstanding wife for any man in her village, but I am forgetting that there are no eligible men in her village or in any village like hers. Woman are one-fifth the value of men. They are merely snatched to make up numbers if too many men die on the march back to the coast. 'I could do nothing to help you.' Even as the words fall from my mouth I know that they are the very words she expected to hear. 'You see I have no excuses for my present circumstances, they were thrust upon me and I accepted them. Some years ago a king's trader captured me and sold me to one of their factors. He, in turn, taught me the principles of their language and methods of trading. He seemed loath to allow me to join the coffle, partly on account of my age but also because, as he declared, he could espy some spark of intelligence. When he died (of his addiction to liquor and hot women) I was brought by his under-trading officer to this Fort and subjected to vile abuses until they realized that a replacement factor would not be forthcoming. I subsequently acquired some status in their eyes and began to assist their trading. But now their mode of trading has changed, and civilized gifts are not being proffered, permission to trade in restricted domains not being sought; there are no longer any meetings to interpret and my status has once more fallen off. My soul is not at peace. I sometimes wonder why I do not go with the rest of our people, but I fear what you fear and what we all fear, that there may be awful misery beyond these shores.' I pause. 'I could not help you because I was frightened.' She stares blankly at me and I am unable to tell whether or not she believes a word of what I have just related. She asks me why, if I am so consumed with fear, I risk my situation by bringing her back here. There is much in this question that I cannot answer, but I present her with the simplest explanation. 'You see, I wanted to know what happened between you and Price, for that is the name of the man who came with me on the first journey. What did he do to make you scream? It appears to me as though he took a light and burned small patches of your skin. Is it this that made you scream?' She looks directly at me and does not hesitate with her answer. 'Well, it is this,' she says, 'and more. Yes, he burned me with fire, but he also entered me at the smaller end. Is this something that gives these people pleasure? He seldom spoke with me. For each mark of fire that he made on my body he entered me again but he never seemed to break into satisfaction, do you understand?' I nod, scarcely able to believe what I am hearing. 'And then my mouth, he took pleasure there, but again he could not break into satisfaction and I found it as painful but even more shameful for I could not scream. When he did not like the noise that I would sometimes make when he took pleasure at the back end, he would use my mouth to quieten me and say that if he felt my teeth he would kill me.' 'He did this?' Could Price not see that this is a beautiful and sensitive sixteen-year-old girl, not some whore to whom a broken piece of mirror glass will suffice to purchase any amount of degradation? Maybe he has forgotten the difference, if ever he knew there to be one. I have to control my feelings of anger. 'And did you tell your father of these incidents?' She smiles, her white teeth perfectly uniform in brightness and spacing. 'Of course I did not tell my father. He is a man. In our tradition he is able to give up a daughter more readily than he would his pride or his position in the village. When I returned they asked nothing of me, having already decided that I was unclean. Perhaps they thought my presence would poison others.' The girl tries to remain jovial but it is a simple matter to detect her pain. 'I was sent to a hut on the far side of the village, out of sight and sound of everybody else. I was expected to manage by myself.' She laughs and I encourage her to keep her voice down. 'You see,' she says, this time in a whisper, 'I would almost certainly have died if you had not returned. I have no experience of looking after myself, unlike others who are taught from an early age the use of the spear, shield, and hoe. I was the Head Man's daughter. I had no reason to acquire the skills of hunting or cultivation.' I wonder if her genuine tone is meant to offer up evidence of how grateful she is to me. 'Is there something else you wish to ask?' I sit next to her and take her hand. I hope up that she will not resist. She does not. 'There is nothing further I have to ask of you,' she says 'I have asked questions and you have given me your answers. I do not think that we should exhaust each other with questions that merely repeat what it is that we both already know.' Her wisdom surprises me. I turn my head towards her and kiss her on the mouth. She does not respond but I am keen to explore what I have now tasted. I push her back and lie beside her on the straw. Then I tease one hand around behind her head and kiss her again, and this time her lips are slightly moist and parted, ready to receive me. She entwines me in her arms and legs and I mount and enter her in the right place and deposit myself quickly. She caresses me and makes me feel as though our love-making has been prolonged and exhausting. She falls asleep in my arms. It has often occurred to me that I might have forfeited the right to the emotion of love by virtue of my present situation. I know now that this is not the case. That I can care, that I have the capacity to touch and feel tender, to look after a small child (although she hates me calling her this), shocks me, but makes it possible for me to rediscover some form of self-respect. I shall stop worrying about who might have noticed that the supplies are low, although I will still excuse a caution that is bred of habit. There remains but one worry; the return of the expedition. Their reappearance will make my life more complex, for while it is possible to disguise the presence of the girl with six others present, the return of the expeditionary force will herald the start of my work and the introduction of much vigilance around the Fort. I begin to think about running away with the girl.

❦ CARLENE HATCHER POLITE ❦

# The Flagellants

*Carlene Hatcher Polite currently teaches at SUNY Buffalo. (Sometimes I wonder about all of the great authors who are teaching writing; especially some of the most important ones and most especially about the voices that created the Black Arts Movement in the 1970s—do they really love teaching or do they have to do it to get by?) Although this piece is from* The Flagellants *she has also written another excellent work called* Sister X and the Victims of Foul Play.

"LOVE, YOU BRING ME FULL ROUND TO THE BEGINNING. HIGHNESS, I am again the low, veiled female who, unhanded by you, paused somewhere on the curve of a quiet flux. Having wrongly desired you, Jimson, I must learn how to lose gracefully what I have not found. At this moment, if I had my way, we would be somewhere where it is quiet as the center of the universe. Maybe there would be the sound of the city lending a syncopated pulse to the languid atmosphere. The atmosphere would be permeated with the musk and warmth of an exotic perfume — not too heavy, not too sweet. The scent would arouse the breath

flowing through our nostrils and cause us to go on and on prais-
ing its smell, trying to define its elusive, captivating quality.

"Every object in this dream-room would bespeak a lush, sophisticated, but reverent attitude. There would I be dark brown,
massive, and delicate woods. Colors boldly, fluently, the language of the streets. Your hair and eyes would become crazy,
pitch black, bizarre as the smoke. I would be knocked out by
perception. It is a gas . . . My lips would need constant wetting;
my fingers would lose their nervousness that perplexes me. They
agitate me so much, Jimson. Yes, I would be feeling good now. I
would begin touching flesh—my flesh. I would test its receptiv-
ity. My hands would play in your wild bush of hair, with your
eyebrows. My lips could not stay away from your eyes; my tongue
could not stay away from your nostrils and teeth. Something
would push us closer; only our knees and toes would touch. Our
feet would begin prodding each other. I would toss away from
you. Our voices would make sounds only lovers are able to trans-
late.

"The spell would break itself of its own volition. Blue would
filter down upon us. Sensing the change that has overtaken us,
we would begin plaguing each other with questions. 'What is
the matter?' 'What is wrong?' 'Do you love me?' 'Nothing,' we
would answer. 'Yes, I love you,' we would tell each other, 'a little
bit . . .' You would grab me harshly for saying this to you. Your
body would pierce my bones. We would begin to wrestle with
the blue feeling. Pressing down across our throats, we would feel
its escaping. Water would run off us from every square inch of

skin. You would lift me abruptly, in order to place your hand under my head. Because you have hurt me, I would frown. The flower's spiked petals are dropping one by one. The sunlight stream heats, scorches the floor. The drink belches in our bellies. Whatever it is we would be saying now, we cannot hear. Our ears are being captured by the collective heart. I see the top of your head. My hands direct the shape of your hair. God, your mouth is hot, your tongue a whip. The sharpness of your teeth stings my breast. You begin to suck, mouth, chew them. Ah, Jimson, in this warm, erotic dream, you would drive me crazy, cause me to squirm against all that I desire. Regaining myself, I kiss your heart, your breast. I would kiss them as you would like, my love, never allowing them to get cold, so that the room's wind would fall upon them, coldly breaking our enchantment. The motion of our heads would begin reacting in our backs. Our senses would be directed toward our pointed beings. Our mouths would open wet, coming down fast. Teeth would bring us back into the room. Whatever you are saying again, I would not hear. We would know that it is the mood, the time of life; that is enough. Come on, now . . .

"In this same moment, I am out of it. All I know is nothing. What I would witness would make me stop breathing. Your mouth is a leech taking the blood out of me. Your teeth would clinch my spirit, while your tongue mopped my soul. My eyelids would part with tears. Everything would stiffen, yearn to cry out. Nothing would come but a groan and a dying sigh. Yes, it is feeling good as we try to procreate the absolute orgasm, the crucifixion. Death is the complete, ultimate release. We would attack each other, kiss, lick, and suck the life out of each other. Vampirically, sweat would blot up the sheets. We cannot stand it any more. I beg you to please just let me be, let me rest, find my bearings. I would plead, 'Stop this nonsense.' You would look at me as if I were a perfect stranger. My voice could not say your name. Who are you? What are you doing to me? The arrested moment would take too long. Irritated, impatient, I would feel your presence lower itself down upon me. O, God. O, my goodness . . . Ouch! Probing, it starts to plumb, push, thrust. Grunting, stammering, gasping, we swallow salty saliva. You shout that I do something, say something. What would you want me to say?

"Yes. Come on now, sweet lover, love me hurt me. Yes, it feels good. Stop! Yes, I love you. Help! Yes, you are my man. Please . . . Let me be your slave. Make me lose my mind. Let me just die. Quit! Kill me. Yes . . . Nails would plunge into your flesh. Our lips would bump into each other's. We would become our black dog, lapping it up. Wings would flutter. Snakes would hiss. Oh, we cannot help ourselves. Eyes would turn away. In the next moment, I would hear your voice lowering to make its pronouncement. My flesh would choke you, tensing for the moment. Muscles would gargle and grind, stretching toward IT. Then it would begin to ease. Your voice is distinct, each syllable rings emphatically. Our beings, extending infinitely, would come to the end of their missions as we absorb the sensation of having realized the spirit of union. The unborn world spurting tears, shooting off, would wash our old souls with a bewildering divine jangle. An angel would receive its wings. Then our beings would give us back to ourselves. Our gazes would meet to question our identities and the state which we naturally visited . . . just now."

## ❧ PATRICIA POWELL ❧

# The Pagoda

*Patricia Powell was born in Jamaica in 1966 and received her education at Wellesley College (B.A.) and Brown University (M.F.A. in Creative Writing). Her novels include* Me Dying Trial, A Small Gathering of Bones, *and* The Pagoda.

ONE NIGHT HE HAD A DREAM THAT MISS SYLVIE HAD COME TO HIS bed, and when he woke up he was frightened to find her lying there next to him and even more alarmed to find that his spindly arm was trapped underneath her wide shoulders, and he tried to remove it at once, though stealthily so as not to wake her. It was impossible, though she slept without peace, with outstretched arms and churning fingers, with a face gashed by nightmares and a heaving chest that sometimes produced a deep rattle from her throat. Thin strands of yellow hair swiveled off her freckled cheeks and the fragile limb that was her brown throat. He had never seen a beauty quite like this and so close up to him and so overwhelmingly feminine and ripe and bursting it confused him. Frightened him, really. Even the way she smelled, as if frothing, and there was the taste of her sweat firing. Out from the barbs of bush that were her underarms.

It was early morning and streaks of light were already peering in through the chinks in the red velvet curtain and outside he could hear the stirring call of cocks and the response of other cocks from deep down in the valley on the other side of the rolling gray hill, and he heard too the warbling of swallows, the cooing of doves, the crying of chickadees, the whirring of hummingbirds, more cock calls. Slowly he turned his head so as to make out the location of his shoes on the rug near the door that would lead him down the hall, past the neighboring room, the gilded frames of handsome and romantic landscapes of regions he did not know, the low narrow chest of drawers, the well-made bed with unruffled sheets and balloon pillows, past the window that looked out at the kitchen, and then the door, finally the door that would bring him escape. It was too much, this . . . this . . . he didn't even know what to call it, his yearning was so furious.

She cleared her throat and Lowe saw that a rectangle of sun had hoisted across the room and leaned into her face and that she was wide awake and watching him with amused eyes still drugged by sleep, and he immediately freed his thin white arm that had long gone dead. He lurched toward his shoes, and she stopped him with the narrative of how she had been married since she was fifteen and within months after the dreams started coming her husband fell off his horse and broke his neck.

"But every night it was your face I keep seeing," she told

Lowe, in a voice touched with tenderness. "How that to happen so?" she whispered, tracing the bones of his cheeks with the pads of her fingers, running them along the rugged lines of his lips, gently removing the black band of hair that lay there, circling the eyes and the curve of his nostrils, all the while singing the music of idle words, minuets about beauty. "Is the same round face with the one eye slightly bigger and the same mouth with the lips so full and pink and with the top one a little longer, the same teeth at the front caved in slightly. My husband used to travel, and I thought maybe it was his sketches that brought the dreams night after night. But it was you, you ownself. For two years."

Lowe fretted under her touch, his body stiff and unmoving, his breath barely able to escape his wildly beating heart, his roaring head. She knew! So then where the hell were the shoes! For if he could slip slightly to the right he would be free of her cream thigh sheathed in black garter that was the stumbling block in his path, he would be ready at the side of the bed and on the floor with the tap-tap of nimble feet down the darkened corridors with only creases of light to guide him through the maze of rooms, past the office with an untidy desk cluttered with papers, short squat chairs and a plush rug, the glimmering edges of a scrubbed floor. With her eyes closed, and with the steaming flesh, she straddled him. His great swooping copper bird with the dazzled gaze, the frenzied admiration, repeating her prosody of love.

Yet underneath her hands, plying his body, awakening it, her attentive fingers listening to it for harmony, there was only discord, for his body would not obey, would not dance, was not flexible and yielding, had no discipline. Above him, there was only the broiling cauldron of sky, a streak of light across a suction sea, a glittering dusk, an unreflecting mirror. Her butterfly kisses feathered his throat, and he was drenched in his own sweat and the fragrances of oils and perfumes, the harsh wet smell of tobacco, that clung to her skin. He felt her wet lips on his wide-open eye, on his sweep of lashes, on a perturbed forehead. A nibble on the lobe of an ear. A stab to the center of the throat with a pointed pink tongue. An ocean of moans. Hers? And then steps silent as a priest's on the rug and wood floors, to his little room at the back of the shop. The naked and unpainted concrete walls of his shop. The shimmering zinc roofs. The awful singing of men. The cracked laughter of men. Laughs deep with disappointments, muddied with mockery, bridled with bitterness. The wooden shelves tiered to the white ceiling with boxed and tinned goods.

There were her teeth tight on the buttons of his shirt, picking them off, one by one. From the hollow of his throat to the thimble of his navel, she roamed with the freckled tongue, with a bow and with a nod. She removed the strips of cloth that banded the chest and swallowed at once the knobby red nipples. She murmured into his chest. She knew! She murmured into his belly. She knew! He continued to lie there dead, columns of tears leaking out the wrinkled corners of his eyes. There were only teeth and hard bites and spread legs and splayed fingers and darting tongue, a valley of breasts, a whirlpool of desire, a feverish breathlessness, a profuse talk of love, words racing and running and leaping, tumbling overhead, there was the chaos of phrases, a dark loamy earth, and Miss Sylvie at his feet, picking off socks, a warm mouth, a gaping cave, swallowing one by one, then the whole bunch, crumpled up.

A gasp for air. His? Fingers on the cracked leather of belt, on the hook of trousers, then on the buttons, and frenzied fingers rummaging into the square white band of his drawers and scrambling up again to wrestle with a wrinkled shirt the color of khaki, then down again, swimming into the white waist and plunging in, a pointed tip of European nose, a taste, finger by finger, then the whole fist crammed in. A ship. A square canvas edge of sail. A checkered oilcloth and the strange curve of flesh. Haggard breathing. Cecil's! The galloping rhythm of tongue, taste of brine on lips, a raised arm with torn wrist a vague twilight and dreamy eyes gripped by the drug of sleep. A molten sky. An auspicious moon. A sweltering marketplace. A circling shark with a murderous tail. A leaning body full of erratic gestures, the undulation of limbs, the crunching of figures, the movement of light. Lowe could not retain the sequence from the chaos.

And so it continued for all those years, Miss Sylvie returning again and again to their room after spending weeks or months at a time with Whitley, who came to visit and who satiated the passion that she must have sought only in Lowe. And Lowe not moving, not rising to her touch or to touch her, not returning her kisses, her pronouncements of love, just lying there numb all those years, for each time, all he could think of was the dark dank of the place, a flash of bruised light, a pair of pliers, an unleashed fury, a strange curve of flesh, and those shoes, ripping through rooms, past the varnished wood of the table, the marbled chests. Secretly and in his heart he yearned for her embrace, and often he wished he could simply small himself up into her lap and sleep there. But always she wanted more. He heard it in her frenzied breathing, he could smell it like danger on her skin, he could taste it at the back of his throat, and it was always there in the pressure of her fingers kneading him. He didn't feel as if he had agency, as if he had voice. For who is to say she wouldn't fold up her fantasies into him and turn him further into something he wasn't, as his father had done and then Cecil? And who is to say she wouldn't abandon him once her mission was accomplished. Who is to say!

And so Lowe just lay there prostrate, so overwhelmed by his fear, allowing Miss Sylvie to love him, those nights after Cecil had come, and left again, those nights after Whitley had gone, those nights after Liz had gone to sleep, and later, after she had eloped with the carpenter and escaped the convent school, which only as an exception admitted the children of the Chinese and those of the porcelain alabasters, those nights after the store had prospered and he had expanded and met Kywing, those nights when it was just the two of them, just the two of them and the dark and impenetrable night.

And for all those years Lowe had never wanted to touch her in that way, never wanted to love her in that way, never wanted to stroke the lines on her forehead or the ones by the corners of her eyes and lips. For who is to say what he would have raised up in her! He had never wanted to touch the mole on her back or the one on the right side of her neck, never wanted to inspect the insides of her legs or thighs, never wanted to fondle her nipple, never wanted to possess her body or snatch her from the claws of that woman, never wanted to kiss her parted lips or the smooth column of throat, never wanted to smell her perfumed skin or to taste her sea-salt silkiness, never wanted to travel inside her, never wanted to crawl or push, never wanted, never wanted till that moment. For at that moment he was a child not so afraid of death, and of darkness and of solitude. At that moment he was a child full up of innocence, ebullient with faith.

# Somethin' Extra

*Patty Rice is cofounder of My Sister Writers, an authors' group for African-American women. As a poet she has published a chapbook,* Manmade Heartbreak, *and as a novelist she's written* Somethin' Extra. *She currently resides in Maryland with her two daughters where she is at work on her second novel.*

I DECIDED TO STRIP OFF MY CLOTHES. THE SKIRT AND VEST CAME off. I unbuttoned my top and flung it on the floor. Unhooked my bra and let that fall, then stepped out of my panties. I took the bobby pins out of my hair and shook it out. Then I marched myself down the hall to David's bedroom. He was already in the shower. His non-singing behind was in there grooving to "My Girl," except he was saying "my Genie." David loved to change the words to songs.

I busted right in that bathroom like Norman Bates would have and pulled back the shower curtain. There was so much steam in there I could hardly breathe. David had soap everywhere on his chest. His hair was slick and dark. His beautiful penis and those long hairy legs were glistening and dripping water.

He looked so damn good I just wanted to rinse him off with my tongue. He was looking at me like he was surprised and didn't really want me in there, so I got all shy like an idiot and started fiddling with the shower curtain. You would have thought I was a virgin or something.

"Can I join you?" I asked him, looking down. The water from the shower curtain was hitting my feet and getting all over the floor. David put out his hand. I took it and stepped inside the tub in front of him. He adjusted the water for me, because it was a little too hot, and when he got it just right, I let the spray douse my hair and run down my body. It felt so good. I reached behind me and pulled David's arms around me so his hands could cup my breasts, but when he hesitated, I turned around to look up at him.

"You sure you want me?" he asked.

"You still want me?" I was scared of what he would say, but he looked at me like I was crazy and said, "Always. I just thought you needed to . . . I don't know. I thought I should wait until you told me you were ready to again."

That made me laugh. I moved all the way up against his chest.

"Doc, you mean to tell me we've both been missing out for nothing?"

"I guess," he said.

"Well, let me say this plainly. I'm more than ready."

I stood on my tiptoes to kiss him. The man lifted me and pinned me to the shower wall, barely giving me enough time to wrap my legs around him before he was inside me, making my head spin.

◄| NTOZAKE SHANGE |►

# Liliane: Resurrection
# of the Daughter

*Multi-talented Ntozake Shange has won acclaim as a playwright*
(for colored girls who have considered suicide/when the rainbow
is enuf), *a poet* (The Love Space Demands), *and a novelist* (Betsey
Brown *and* Sassafras, Cypress & Indigo). *This selection is from* Liliane: Resurrection of the Daughter, *which is, I think, her best
novel, and one of my top ten books of 1994.*

LILIANE'S FAVORITE STORY, WHEN SHE WAS DRIPPING AND NAKED,
especially if she was tremblin' and holdin' me so she wouldn't
leap off the bed, her favorite story was about a young girl at the
Corso for the first time. This is how it goes. Once upon a time a
young girl, a pretty young girl, *una morena*, bronze like you with
the piquancy of a ginger flower, adorned herself in organdy and
silk. She tugged at a very loud garter belt and slowly wound
brand-new stockings up her long legs. She stuffed taffeta slip
upon taffeta slip neath the swing of her skirts and giggled at herself in the mirror, dabbing rose lipstick from one end of her

smile to the other. She put her lovely feet, toes wigglin' to dance, she put them toes in a pair of fancy cloth shoes with rhinestone butterflies twirlin' about her heels. Yes, she did. Then she tossed a velvet shawl round her shoulders and was off to the Corso.

The East Side train was not quite an appropriate carriage for such a *flaca tan linda*, but she rode the ske-dat-tlin' bobbin' train as if it were the *QE 2*. At 86th Street she ran into a mess of young brothahs who callt to her, whispered, whistled, circled her, ran up behind her, got close enough to smell her, made her change her direction once or twice, til they realized she was determined to walk up the steps to the Corso and they couldn't, cause they had rubber-soled shoes. We all knew you can't wear rubber-soled shoes on the glorious floor of the Corso. So, *cariña*, the young girl who looked so beautiful, she looked almost as lovely as you do now, *chica*. She sashayed by the bar, through the tables crowded with every kinda Latin ever heard of, and stationed herself immediately in front of *El Maraquero* in the aqua lamé suit. *Oigame, negreta*. His skin was smooth as a star-strewn *portegria* night, see, like me, *negra*. Put your hand right there by my chin. Now, his bones jut through this face with the grace of Arawak deities. Like that, see. Now, run your fingers through my mustache *porque* his lips blessed the universe with a hallowed, taunting voice; high, high *como* a cherub, yes, a Bronx boy on a rooftop serenading his *amante, sí*. The way I speak to you, now, *sí*. This young girl was mesmerized. She was how you say when you bein' *bourgesa*, "smitten," right? No, don't move your fingers from my lips, not yet. But the most remarkable feature of *el maraquero*, what did her in, as we say, had the young pussy justa twitchin', ha, was *el ritmo* of the maracas in his hands. Ba-ba-ba/baba . . . Ba-ba-ba/baba. Oh, she could barely stand the tingling sounds so exact every beat, like an unremitant, *mira*, an unremitant, waterfall Ba-ba-ba/baba . . . Ba-ba-ba/baba . . . Ba-ba-ba/baba. Oh, she started to dance all by herself. It was as if your folks said the Holy Ghost done got holdt to her. She was flyin' round them bambos, introducing steps the Yorubans had forgotten about. She conjured the elegance of the first *danzón* and mixed it with twenty-first-century Avenue D salsa. The girl was gone. No, *dulce*, don't move your fingers. Here, let me kiss them. One by one. Cause that's what happened to the beautiful mad dancin' girl and our *maraquero*. For she was so happy movin' to the music he was makin' and she imagined he meant for this joy to overwhelm her. She started to cry ever so slightly. Let me kiss the other one. No not that one, the littlest one. With all her soul she thought he was tossin' those maracas through the air for her. So naturally her tears fell on the beat. No, don't laugh. Listen. Listen. The tears fell from her cheeks slowly and left aqua lamé streaks on her cheeks. Really. Then once they hit the floor; it was like a bolt of lightning hit *El Maraquero*, who jumped into an improvisation whenever one of them tears let go of that girl's body. Soon it was she who was keepin' *el ritmo* and he was out there on some *maraquero's sueño* of a solo. Now you know, *El Maraquero* has to be disciplined. He's gotta control, oh, the intricacies of Iberian and West African polyrhythms as they now exist in salsa music, right? Okay, let me have the other hand. No, I want to lick the palm of your other hand or I can't finish the story.

You want me to finish the story, don't you? Well, good. Now I'll have kissed all your fingers and your palms and the bend in your arm. So *El Maraquero* became agitated. He wanted to know where his sound had gone, and to be honest so did the rest of the orchestra Well, *he* hadn't noticed our beautiful young girl in her slips and organdy, her shoes with twirlin' butterflies. He wasn't like me, huh, he didn't see the surrender in her dancin' to his music. So he was astonished when he went to play and no sound came from the maracas. Our young girl, Liliane, who was so much like you, saw what he felt and she knew as he did not know that you do not own the beauty you create. Right, hear me. You don't own the beauty. Oh, I wanta kiss one of those rose tits of yours. No, I'm not finished with the story. Yes, let me nearer. No, don't move your fingers. *El Maraquero* is fuming. The young girl who's been dancin' and crying all filled up with something she can't call by name 'cept to say that she likes it. She starts cryin' inconsolably cuz *El Maraquero* has lost his music and she doesn't know where it is 'cept that not owning beauty doesn't mean you lose it. Well, let's see that finger again. No, I want the next one. No don't rush me. The young girl runs toward him and he's really pissed. I mean, no, I'm not pissed, I'm lickin' you, *pendeja*. He doesn't understand that he'll be playing no more music, no nothin', til he accepts that this young girl in her frilly dress and *mariposa* slippers has got holdt to his music. She's so upset about him not tink-tink-tink-tinktinkin' for her. Out of *desesperación* she starts to sing to him and one by one the seeds that had been her tears that had been her legs and hips dancin' to his *ritmo* all returned to the maracas and *El Maraquero* never lost sight of her again. Turn over. From then on, *negrita*, he played for his life every *cancion*, *cada coro*, cause his *chabala* would dance and cry his *ritmo* for him and then give it all back with her tears, her tears from feelin' what she had no name for, had never felt before, and couldn't do without. Right, Liliane, isn't that how it is for you?

Oh, she'd jump up and call me every lowdown exploitative muthafuckah in the world. It was "*chingathis*" and "*chingathat.*" "I'll be damned if it ain't some sick-assed voyeuristic photographer thinks his art is nurtured by a woman's tears." "Suck, it, niggah," she'd scream, or sometimes she said, "Suck it, spic," if she was really mad. Then she'd turn around, tryin' to dress herself in this state. Something was always on backward or she, put on mismatched shoes, threw my hat on her head steada mine. She'd go stormin' out saying, "My art is not dependent on fuckin' you or hurtin' you. Niggah, my art ain't gotta damn thing to do with your Puerto Rican behind. Besides you can't take pictures, anyway. Go study with Adal Maldonado, you black muthafuckah."

That's when I could watch her go down the avenue, wet and smellin' exactly how I left her. Then I watched all the other muthafuckahs just feel how she walked, talkin' under her breath in that butchered Spanish she talks when she's mad at me. I watch them watchin her and I know if I strolled down the street within the next hour I might as well be who I said I was in the beginning: Pete "El Conde" Rodriguez *que toca la música.* Only the instrument I played is named Liliane.

# ⊰ JOHN A. WILLIAMS ⊱

# The Man Who Cried I Am

*John A. Williams was called "arguably the finest Afro-American novelist of his generation" by the* Dictionary of Literary Biography. *He was born in Jackson, Mississippi, in 1925 and attended high school in Syracuse, New York. After serving with the U.S. Navy in the Pacific (1943–1946), he received his B.A. from Syracuse University in 1950. He was a public relations man, English professor, television producer, special assignment writer for more than a dozen American newspapers, and European correspondent for* Ebony *and* Jet *magazines. His major works include* Night Song, The Man Who Cried I Am, Captain Blackman, *and* Sons of Darkness, Sons of Light: A Novel of Some Probability.

SHE KNEW IF THEY DID NOT MAKE LOVE THAT NIGHT, THE MORNING would be unpleasant, and somehow he knew it too, and came softly at her, removing the gown, and she embraced him hard and lovingly with her whiteness, opening all of herself, for she wanted him to know in the fullest way that white could love black and did, and they both sensed that the drunk American downstairs had to be erased with love, and they went from one bed to the other without a pause, a mass of black and white, with arms and legs twisted, their breath coming short above the music from downstairs and Margrit remembered crying silently, her tears mixing unnoticed with the perspiration of their bodies and how, when they left the beds, they drifted across the room to the sun parlor where the full moon leaned patiently against the windows while the sea rushed headlong against the seawall a few hundred yards away downstairs, exploding into billions of phosphorescent bubbles; they put out their cigarettes and began to make love again in a sun parlor chair, lap-love, and the moonlight stroked their restless, jerking bodies, him in her, her around him, moving in that good rhythm until the little cries came again and the pimples rose on their flesh and the nipples of her breasts shot hard and trembling beneath his kneading hands; the exhausted bodies unhinged; they heard the sea withdraw from the wall; the swollen lips parted and Margrit felt a hot, electric quivering down there, a reaction, as she slid from his lap.

And the morning was quite all right.

# ⊲ ACKNOWLEDGMENTS ⊳

Excerpt from *A Harlot's Progress* by David Dabydeen, Copyright © Jonathan Cape. Used by permission of The Random House Group Limited.

Excerpt from *Daughters of the Dust* by Julie Dash, Copyright © 1997 by Geechee Girls Productions, Inc. Used by permission of Dutton, a division of Penguin Putnam Inc.

Excerpt from *Between Lovers* by Eric Jerome Dickey, Copyright © 2001 by Eric Jerome Dickey. Used by permission of Dutton, a division of Penguin Putnam Inc.

Excerpt from *Platitudes* by Trey Ellis, Copyright © by Trey Ellis. Reprinted from *Platitudes* with the kind permission of Trey Ellis.

Excerpt from *Secrets* by Nuruddin Farah, Copyright © 1998 by Nuruddin Farah. Reprinted from *Secrets* published by Arcade Publishing, New York, New York.

Excerpt from *Abide with Me* by E. Lynn Harris, Copyright © 1999 by E. Lynn Harris. Used by permission of Doubleday, a division of Random House, Inc.

Excerpt from *Bone Black* by bell hooks, Copyright © 1996 by Gloria Watkins. Reprinted by permission of Henry Holt and Company LLC.

Excerpt from *Middle Passage* by Charles Johnson, Copyright © 1990 by Charles Johnson. Reprinted with the permission of Scribner, an imprint of Simon & Schuster Adult Publishing Group.

Excerpt from *Mosquito* by Gayl Jones, Copyright © 1999 by Gayl Jones. Reprinted by permission of Beacon Press, Boston.

Excerpt from *The Cotillion, or, One Good Bull Is Half the Herd* by John Oliver Killens, Copyright © 1971 by John Oliver Killens.

Reprinted with the permission of Coffee House Press, Minneapolis, Minnesota.

Excerpt from *The Autobiography of My Mother* by Jamaica Kincaid, Copyright © 1996 by Jamaica Kincaid. Reprinted by permission of Farrar, Straus and Giroux, LLC.

Excerpt from *All-Night Visitors* by Clarence Major, Copyright © by Clarence Major. Used by permission of Clarence Major and The John Talbot Agency.

Excerpt from *Praisesong for the Widow* by Paule Marshall, Copyright © 1983 by Paule Marshall. Used by permission of G.P. Putnam's Sons, a division of Penguin Putnam Inc.

Excerpt from *Sugar* by Bernice L. McFadden, Copyright © 2000 by Bernice L. McFadden. Used by permission of Dutton, a division of Penguin Putnam Inc.

Excerpt from *Jazz* by Toni Morrison, Copyright © 1992 by Toni Morrison. Reprinted by permission of International Creative Management, Inc.

Excerpt from *The Seven League Boots* by Albert Murray, Copyright © 1995 by Albert Murray. Used by permission of Pantheon Books, a division of Random House Inc.

Excerpt from *The Women of Brewster Place* by Gloria Naylor, Copyright © 1980, 1982 by Gloria Naylor. Used by permission of Viking Penguin, a division of Penguin Putnam Inc.

Excerpt from *It Begins with Tears* by Opal Palmer Adisa, Copyright © by Opal Palmer Adisa. Reprinted by permission of Harcourt Education Publishers.